RUTHIE'S LOVE

A MORGAN'S RUN ROMANCE

M. LEE PRESCOTT

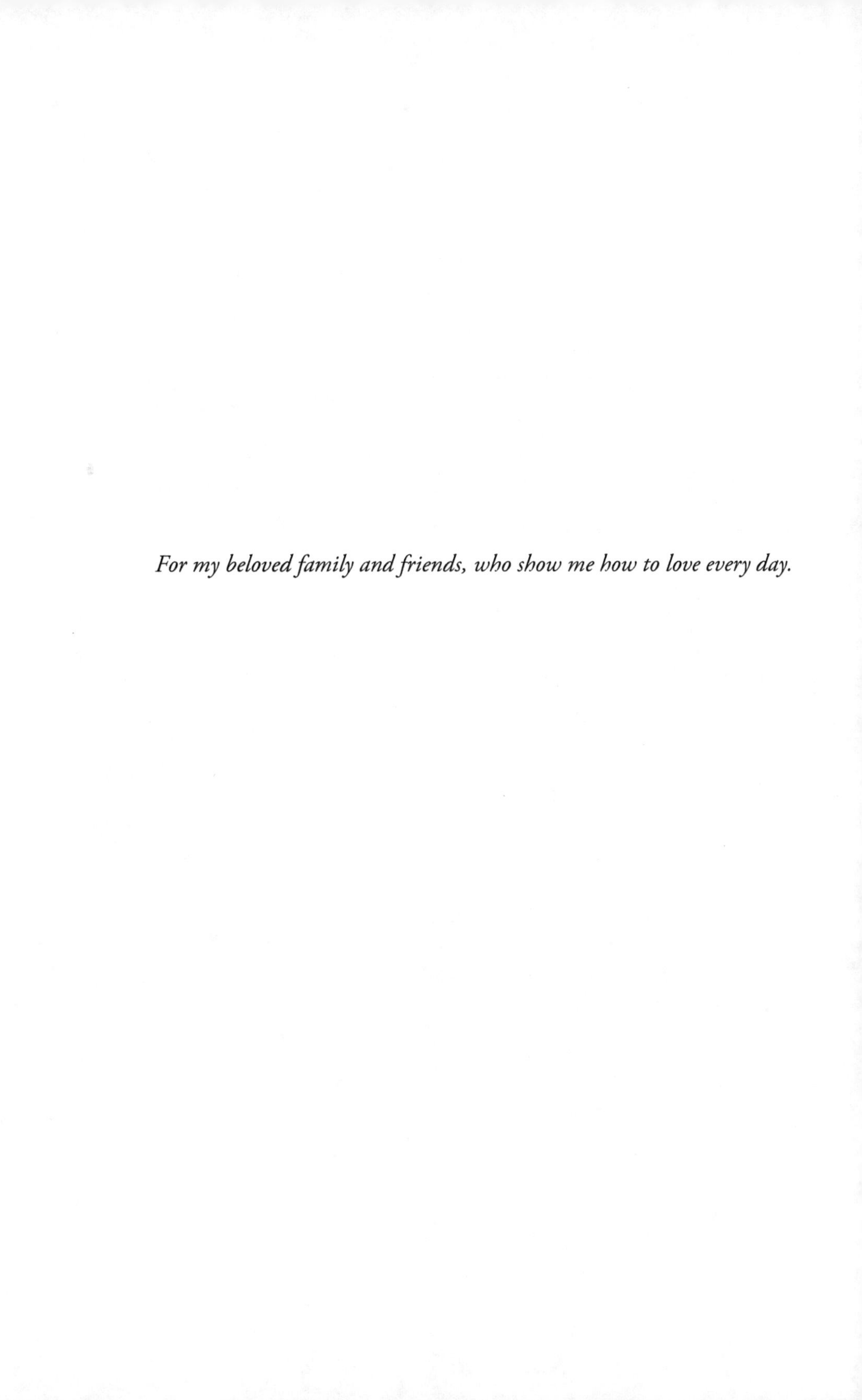

For my beloved family and friends, who show me how to love every day.

CHAPTER 1

An early summer breeze blew through open windows as Harley Langdon gazed around at the place he'd called home for fifteen years. After a brief stint in a ranch cabin, he had respectfully declined his employers' many offers to live on Morgan's Run. He loved them—they were his family—but he preferred his own space in town. Now as he contemplated the big move, he was surprised at how nostalgic he felt.

California was a long way from the Valley. Except for college, he had spent his entire life in Saguaro Valley. He knew everyone in town and they knew him. His best friend, Ben Morgan, was here, as were his coworkers, all of them good friends. The Morgan family had embraced him when his own family fell apart. His parents were both gone and his only sister, Carrie, lived in Boise.

Telling family patriarch, Ben Morgan Senior, about the job offer had been one of the hardest things he'd ever done. In true Morgan style, his boss had congratulated him and been genuinely happy for him. General manager of Hayworth Ranch was a dream job and represented a tremendous opportunity, well-suited to Harley's background and expertise. Much as he loved the Valley and its people, the chance to breed and train champion race horses was something he would never have at Morgan's Run.

As he threw books into a box, he glanced over at his dresser, where several photos were displayed. His fifteen-year-old daughter, Willow, smiled from the nearest. Next to her was a shot of the stable crew taken before a recent riding exhibition—Maggie Morgan, Ben's wife, their assistant, Jeb Barnes, horse trainer Nick Parker, and several of the college kids who worked part-time for them. Harley had his arm around Maggie. Beautiful, strong Maggie. The last picture was of the entire Morgan family taken the previous winter at a wedding.

His gaze lingered on the youngest Morgan daughter, who leaned on a crutch, broken leg in a cast. "You'll be better off without me, kiddo."

As he turned away from the woman he loved, his cell phone rang. "Mornin', Harley, how you doin'?"

Surprised to hear Ben Senior's voice, he said, "Great, sir. I'm just headed to the barn."

Ben Morgan laughed. "I'm not checkin' up on you, son. I've got a favor to ask."

"Anything, shoot."

"What's your day like?"

"Usual stuff. Organizing supply orders for the pack trip, lessons. You know the drill."

"Any chance you'd let an old man take you to lunch?"

"Sure, you got it."

"Good, meet you in town around noon, unless later's better?"

"Noon'd be fine," he said, shaking his head as they made arrangements and rang off. He had shared hundreds of meals with the Morgans over the years, but he couldn't ever remember having lunch with the big boss. *What is this about?*

CHAPTER 2

Ruthie Morgan bounced into the dining room and hugged her father on her way to the breakfast laid out on the sideboard.

"Carmela made strawberry pancakes, your favorite. Be sure to thank her," her mother said, referring to their housekeeper, who had been with the family since her teens.

"Like I wouldn't. You guys are up early," her daughter said. "Dad, you coming to the farm for lunch today?"

"Not today, Sweet Pea."

"But, you come every Thursday!"

"I know, darlin'. Can I have a rain check till tomorrow?"

Her mother, Leonora, brushed a lock of blonde hair from her forehead as she frowned across the table at her daughter. "Don't pout, Ruthie Ann. It's very unbecoming."

Ruthie rolled her eyes. "It's also unbecoming to scold your adult daughter."

"Oh, pish tush. Eat your breakfast and off you go. I'm sure your sister has been up there for hours."

"Has not. As a matter of fact, your favorite daughter is coming in late today."

"Oh? Nothing wrong, I hope."

"Lily's got a doctor's appointment." Ruthie quickly raised her hand, "Routine, no crisis!"

The two Morgan sisters ran the ranch's farm, one of the largest organic operations in the Southwest. Ruthie ran the farm and gardens and Beth, her older sister, took care of the office and oversaw the processing of produce and meats. Raoul, Carmela's husband, and his men managed the livestock.

The Cottage can't be completed soon enough!" Leonora said, referring to the child care facility the elder Morgans were building on the ranch for their grandchildren. "I wish Hope was still with them." Hope Seymour, a dear friend of Beth's who was engaged to their brother Robbie, had been acting as nanny for Beth and Lang's baby daughter, Lily.

"Now, Nora, she'll be back in a couple of weeks. She's getting her affairs in order before Sam and Rose's wedding." In a few short weeks, their second eldest child would marry Rose Dillon, daughter of their dear friends and neighbors.

"I know, I know, but she's been gone for over a month. So hard on poor Bethie."

Ruthie frowned at her mother. "Beth is fine. Lang's around and Lily's a good baby. Oh, my God, Carmela, these pancakes are amazing!" She shouted toward the kitchen door.

"Ruthie Ann, please, lower your voice!"

Ben Senior sat back smiling at two of his favorite women. His hot-headed redhead and the gorgeous blonde he married forty years ago. To his eyes, his college sweetheart grew lovelier every day and his baby girl was no longer a child. Her freckles had faded and her round face was now thinner. *My cute little girl has blossomed into a lovely woman.*

"Why can't you come to lunch anyway?" Ruthie asked, interrupting his reverie.

"Got business in town."

"What kind of business?" Leonora asked. "You never said."

"Odds and ends."

Both mother and daughter turned to stare at him.

"What kind of a ridiculous answer is that?" Leonora said.

"Can't a fella be mysterious now and then?"

His wife set down her coffee mug. "Ben Morgan, when have you ever been mysterious? What are you up to? If it involves going to that greasy spoon taco shack on the Gila with Spark, the answer is no. You promised to eat healthy!"

"I'm not going out for tacos, darlin', but can't promise I won't run into my best buddy along the way."

Leonora waved her hand in dismissal. "Oh, have your secrets. I've got Cowbelles this morning and it's our planning meeting for the auction, so I'll be gone till after one. I want to stop by the Cottage, too, and see when Carmela and I can get in there with the furnishings. They delivered another huge truckload of things yesterday. "

"Gonna be somethin'," he said.

"Then I'm off to the airport. You know your Aunt Helen arrives today, Ruthie?"

"Yup, be great to see her. Is there a reason she's coming west?"

"A large commission in Scottsdale. She's already shipped the windows, but she wants to supervise their installation." Helen Winthrop was actually a cousin with whom Leonora had become reacquainted when the two met a few years earlier on Leonora's shopping trip to New England. Another firm had designed the stained glass windows in the study of the Big House, but Leonora was always thinking about where else a window might be added and very much wanted Helen to design and build it.

"I asked Polly and Lynn to tonight's dinner so we'll be a large crowd. They're all moved into their condo in town, although I still don't know why they didn't want to take one of the cabins. We could have fixed it up real cute for them."

After many interviews and dozens of candidates, they had recently hired two teachers and caregivers for the Cottage, Polly Granger and Lynn Manguilli. The interview team had included both elder Morgans, Beth, sometimes Maggie, and Spark Foster, Ben Senior's dear friend and former college roommate. Spark had recently settled in the Valley, moving from Portland, Oregon. His daughter, Amy, a physical therapist in Tucson, was married to Jeb Barnes. Amy and Jeb's adopted son, Toby, would be at the Cottage, along with Ben and Maggie's two kids, Emma and Ben, Beth's Lily, and two children of one of the ranch workers. During the school year, Emma, who was eight, attended the local school, but would come to the Cottage in the afternoons. Spark had also hired a full-time aide, Heather Sanchez, for Toby, his grandson, who was in a wheelchair. She would be commuting from Tucson every day.

Polly and Lynn had ordered all the toys, books, school-related resources, and most of the furniture, but Leonora was in charge of furnishing what she called the "Grandparents' Lounge."

"Hello? Privacy?" Ruthie said, rolling her eyes again. "Poll and Lynn are my age. They'd rather be in town where there's at least a little action."

"Don't be ridiculous. What action would they find in Saguaro?"

Ruthie winked at her father. "You never know."

Leonora threw up her hands. "And what are we going to do about our poor Maggie? She's overworked already and our Bennie is a handful. He's my grandson and I adore him, but I've never known such a lively toddler."

"Then you've forgotten the behavior of your own sons," her husband said, chuckling.

"But I wasn't working like poor Maggie."

"Stop calling her poor Maggie," Ruthie said. "She's managing just fine, if you want my opinion."

Leonora gave Ruthie another dismissive wave. "Now Maggie's gonna have to do her work and his. And with Jeb in school, it leaves only Maggie and Nick Parker to run it all." She gazed down the table, ignoring her husband's warning look and the slight shake of his head. "Don't look at me that way. She's got to know sometime."

"Know what?" Ruthie asked, looking from one parent to the other.

"Your childhood crush is abandoning us for the high life in California."

Ruthie stared at her mother. "What are you talking about? Dad, what's she talking about?"

Ben shrugged, smiling at his daughter, but said nothing.

"I'm talking about Harley, of course. He's taken a fancy new job and he's leaving the Valley."

Ruthie's fork clattered to the floor. "Dad, is it true?"

"Of course it's true," her mother said. "Now close your mouth and pick up your fork."

Ignoring the fork, Ruthie popped out of her chair, mouth clamped shut.

"Wait, darlin'," Ben said as she brushed by them both.

"Ruthie Ann, you come right back here when your father's speaking to you!"

"Leave her be, Nora. Let her cool down and digest the news."

"Good luck with that. It's for the best. You know it is. She'll see it someday."

CHAPTER 3

Harley pulled up beside the barn just as Jeb Barnes, his assistant, was heading inside. The younger man paused, waving. "Mornin', boss. Sorry I'm late. Amy had to leave early so I had to wait for Toby's sitter."

He smiled at the wiry, blue-eyed cowboy. "No prob, amigo. As you can see, I'm behind schedule myself. I thought Toby went into Tucson with Amy?"

"He did, but we pulled him out of the Tucson center a few weeks back to get ready to make the transition to the ranch day care. Spark's hired a therapist and aide, so she works with him here, and Amy found a great local sitter."

"How's my man doin' anyway?" Harley asked, thinking how much he would miss watching Toby and Ben's kids grow. There was also his own daughter, Willow, but they had already talked. Willow lived with her mom and grandparents in Flagstaff, so they'd be farther away, but she was excited to visit Napa for long weekends and vacations.

As the two men walked into the barn, a familiar antique green truck flew down the road and screeched to a halt in a cloud of dust. "Someone's in a hurry," Jeb said as Ruthie Morgan leaped from her truck and headed toward them. Ruthie's furious eyes were trained on his boss. Like everyone in the Valley, Jeb was well aware of Harley and Ruthie's feelings for each other. *Uh-oh, trouble in Paradise.*

"That's my cue, boss. I'll see you inside. Mornin' Ruthie!"

Jeb disappeared as Ruthie confronted Harley. "How could you! After all my father and this family have done for you?"

He gazed at the young girl he had known all his life, now grown into a beautiful woman. *When did that happen?* He had loved Ruthie Morgan for most of his life. She had been like a kid sister to him, but now? A nagging voice still said—*too young, too young,* but was she?

"Do you really want to do this, Ruthie?"

"Yes, I do! My father is one of the kindest people in the world and you've basically trampled all over that kindness!"

"Is that what your dad said?"

"What do you think?"

"If it helps, he's known about Hayworth for a while."

"So what!"

"It's gonna work out," he said, green eyes soft as he smiled at her.

"For you, maybe, but what about us?"

"Sweetheart, there isn't any us. You know that. I'm sorry."

"No you're not. You're a big fat jerk! A liar and a jerk!" With that, she turned heel and stalked off, but not before he saw tears in her beautiful blue eyes. He leaned on his truck, watching as she peeled out of the lot, jaw set, looking straight ahead. *You're a shit, Harley Langdon,* he thought as he shielded his eyes from the dust.

A few minutes later he was sitting in the barn office, making lists for the day, when his partner, Maggie Morgan, walked in. Motherhood and marriage suited her. His best friend's wife grew lovelier each year. Her thick chestnut hair was tied back in a ponytail, shoved under a faded baseball cap, and her worn jeans hugged her curvaceous figure. A blue ranch tee shirt was stretched tight over her full breasts.

"Mornin', Harl," she said. "I just passed Ruthie going like a bat outta hell. Did she come from here?"

"Yup."

"You guys have a fight?"

"Sit down, Mags. I have something to tell you. Ben doesn't even know yet. I should have said something to both of you much earlier." A man of few words, he wasted none in relating his news as Maggie listened with wide eyes.

"Wow, knock me over with a feather, partner! I mean, I always wondered if this day would come, but yikes, what'll we do without you?"

"Come on, Mags, I'm your boss in name only. We all know you run this place."

"Let me rephrase—what will my husband do without you?"

He grinned. "I expect he'll survive."

"Poor Ruthie. She must be devastated."

"She'll get over it."

"But will you?"

He gave her a look. "Just I'll have to, I guess."

"Harley, are you sure about this? I know it's a great opportunity, but this is your home."

"I'm in a rut, Mags. Have been for a while. You know I love the Valley and all of you. It's just time to try something new. Make a life for myself and for Willow. Her mom's doing good right now, but that won't last. Her treatments cost a fortune. This'll let me contribute more."

"Well, you know you have my support two hundred percent. Maybe once you're settled, Ben and I'll come for a visit?"

"I'd love that."

"Does the job come with housing?"

He nodded. "Three-bedroom house. It's pretty incredible. Mountain views to the east and distant view of the ocean to the west."

She flashed him one of her beautiful smiles that made his best friend go weak at the knees. "That's settled. We're definitely visiting!"

"Thanks, Mags."

"For what?"

"For not telling me I'm a shit."

She reached over and touched his arm. "It's *your* life, Harley Langdon, and don't let any of the Morgans tell you otherwise or make you feel guilty. We'll miss you, absolutely, but we're so proud of you. Geography doesn't change family ties. We'll never lose touch. And don't forget Spark's corporate jet he's always begging us to use."

"There is that."

"It's going be fine. *We're* going to be fine."

"Promise?"

She stood. "Promise. Now, I've got to get to work. You too."

CHAPTER 4

Ben Morgan the second spent the morning at the Lodge, the ranch's luxurious inn and spa. He and his brother Robbie shared duties there, although everyone agreed that Ben was a much better schmoozer. This morning the handsome brothers had been meeting with Jim Thompson, the Lodge manager, and his assistant, Bebe Corcoran, who oversaw the housekeeping staff. Also at the meeting were Mel Farrell and her partner, Rita Lazares, who ran the Spa. They were preparing for the arrival of a large party of twenty-four in five days, ten of whom would taking a pack trip with Ben and Harley as leaders. The other members of the group were scheduled for spa treatments and day excursions. Hope Seymour, Robbie's fiancée, was also teaching three painting classes during their stay. The chance to work with the renowned Southwestern painter had been a major selling point for this group.

"I think we've covered it all," Jim Thompson said, deferring to his bosses. "Unless I've forgotten something?"

Ben Morgan stood up. "Thanks, Jim. As always, you're on top of everything. Now I have to get Harley geared up for the pack trip. At least some of this group have had riding experience."

"So they say," Robbie said. "You know how the last gang of 'experienced riders' turned out. We practically lost two off Carter Ridge."

"Don't remind me," his brother said.

Mel laughed, a deep, throaty chuckle. Strong and athletic with waist-length brown hair, and charcoal eyes, she favored untucked shirts and jeans. Today she wore a faded blue work shirt and shorts. "It's really generous of Hope to be offering the classes. We've got the studio all set up."

Robbie grinned, flashing the drop-dead gorgeous Morgan smile. "She's happy to do it. She'll be back day after tomorrow in plenty of time."

Rita nodded. "And I can assist, if she needs me." A slender blonde, Rita was Mel's partner of many years in life and business. She taught most of the Spa's exercise classes, including the wildly popular hot yoga sessions.

Ben gazed at his companions. "Well, mi amigos, gotta hightail it. Bro, I'm stoppin' at the barn, then I'll be at camp." He referred to Emma's Dream, the camp for handicapped children that he and Maggie had started several years earlier.

"Camp starts soon, huh?" Mel asked.

"Two weeks."

"How is that going to work with the pack trip?" Jim said.

"Robbie and Maggie have things covered," he said. "Don't you, bro?"

"Yup, no prob."

Jim laughed, running a hand over his nearly bald head. "Do you Morgans ever sleep?"

"We're a well-oiled machine, buddy. Gotta be with the bosses lookin' over our shoulders."

"From our vantage point, your dad seems very happy to hand over the reins," Jim said. "And your mom has so many projects, we can't keep 'em straight. She's got us making a hundred boxed lunches for the camp's Opening Day."

"Good. It was too much for Carmela last year. Lunch really helps as Johnny and his staff are gearing up for the dinner. See you all."

The brothers hopped into Ben's Rover. When they pulled up to the barn, Ben frowned. Robbie's truck was parked next to Maggie's jeep and Jeb's old clunker truck.

"Where the hell is Langdon? I told him we needed to go over things this morning."

"Probably running an errand."

The brothers headed in and through the empty barn. All the horses were out, stalls open and laid with fresh sawdust. Rip and Sandy, two of the college students they hired for the summer, were taking the last wheelbarrows of yesterday's sawdust out to the compost area. Ben and Robbie nodded to the guys as they headed out to the stable yard. Nick Parker and Jeb Barnes were in separate corrals, giving lessons, while Maggie stood talking to a woman and young girl who appeared to have just completed a lesson. She waved to them, finished her conversation, and came to greet them.

"Hey, gorgeous," Ben said, drawing her to him for a peck on the cheek.

"Hey, not in front of the kids. Hi, Robbie."

Ben's beautiful wife smiled at her brother-in-law. Not for the first time, Robbie thought how lucky his big brother was. *Still looks a goddess after two kids.* "Hey, Mags. Busy here today, huh? Where can I help?"

"Thanks, Robbie, but I think we're covered. It's going to be a lot busier soon."

"Where the hell is Langdon?" Ben asked. "He and I were gonna meet this morning."

"He'll be back later," she said, eyes studying him. "You two got time to sit for a minute?"

All three grabbed waters from the cooler and sat in the shade. "What's up, hon?" Ben asked. "If Harley's not here, I gotta get over to camp."

Maggie gulped, well aware that this would be the last peaceful conversation she would have with her sometimes hot-headed husband for the foreseeable future. "There's been a development."

Both men gave her puzzled looks.

"As in?" Robbie asked.

"As in Harley," she said, afraid to look her husband in the eye. Finally, she swallowed and looked up. "Sweetheart, Harley wanted to tell you himself, but you weren't here this morning."

"Tell me what?"

"He's leaving Morgan's Run."

"What!"

"Wow," Robbie said as he and Maggie gazed at his brother, waiting for the explosion.

Maggie put a hand on Ben's arm. "Now, stay calm. He's taken a job in Napa as general manager at Hayworth Ranch. It's a big deal and a huge promotion for him."

"We had lunch two days ago. He didn't say a thing."

"I guess he just learned about it. Your dad's known for a while that Harley was in the running for the job, but Harley asked him not to say anything. I'm sure your dad was praying he'd have a change of heart."

Ben stood up and began pacing back and forth. "That ungrateful bastard!"

"Sweetheart, that's not fair and you know it. Harley's been incredibly loyal to this family."

"And we him. This is bullshit! Dad must be devastated. How long have you known?"

"About an hour. Could you please sit down? You'll give yourself a heart attack."

"Does Ruthie know?" Robbie asked.

"Yes, she's already been by."

Robbie whistled. "That must've been ugly."

She gave him a wan smile. "Poor Harley."

"Poor Harley?" Ben asked. "Poor us, you mean! If that's what he's decided, then fuck him!"

"Ben, shush! The clients can hear you!" she said as Jeb said goodbye to a middle-aged woman and headed toward them.

Gazing over at his boss, the young cowboy said, "So, you told him?"

Maggie nodded. "'Fraid so."

"How long have you known?" Ben asked, eyes blazing.

Jeb threw up his hands. "Hey, don't look at me! Just found out today."

"Ben, stop this!" she said. "We—all of us—should be happy for Harley. It's what he's always wanted to do. He'll be in charge of their breeding and training program. That ranch has had some major competitors."

"Where is he?"

"I don't know, but he'll be back in a couple of hours."

"Already checked out, has he?"

"No, and he doesn't intend to go until we find a replacement."

"We don't need a replacement."

"Oh, yes, we do," she said, eyes following her husband as he continued to pace. Underneath the anger, she knew what was really eating him was losing his best friend. Ben and Harley had known each other since nursery school. They'd confided in each other about everything until now. The fact that Harley had kept this from him was as much a reason for the explosion as anything. "While you guys are away on the pack trip, we'll start the process, ask around, send out queries."

"So the turncoat's staying for the trip?"

"Of course he is, and don't call him names. As I just told you, he's staying until we find a replacement. He's already told them at Hayworth."

"Don't do us any favors, Langdon!"

"Ben, that's enough. Let's go in and—"

"I can't talk about this now. Gotta get to camp."

As he stormed off, the others stared at his retreating figure. Ben Morgan never talked to his wife like that.

"Well, that went well, don't you think?" she said, looking from Jeb to Robbie.

Jeb shook his head. "Wouldn't want to be the boss when Ben finds him."

"He'll cool down," she said. "Losing his best friend will be the hardest part for him."

"Want me to talk to him?" Robbie asked.

"Thanks, Rob, but you go on. Didn't I hear they needed you at the farm today?"

"Yup, that's where I am headed. Just checking in and picking up my truck."

"Don't worry, he'll calm down. The kids and I'll plan a fun dinner. That'll take his mind off this."

"Thought everyone was going up to the Big House?"

"Oh, that's right," she said. "That'll be interesting, won't it?"

Robbie nodded as he rose and tossed his empty bottle into the recycle barrel. "See you later, guys."

Maggie laughed. "Yes, you will. Fireworks begin at six."

CHAPTER 5

Harley pulled up beside Ben Morgan Senior's truck. They had agreed to meet in the parking lot beside Gracie's Diner. He jumped out, assuming they would be eating at the popular local diner.

Ben waved but stayed put. "Hey, Harley, hop in. I got Carmela to make us some lunch. Care to take a drive with an old man?"

"Your call, sir."

"And don't start callin' me 'sir' now that you're leavin'. It's taken me decades to break you of that habit."

"Your call, Ben," he said, grinning as he slid into the truck. "Sure you don't want to take my truck?"

"I'm not dead yet, son."

They took the fork at the edge of town, heading north on the Gila Highway. On the west side of the rural highway was Morgan land stretching all the way to the mountains. Most of the land was farm or grazing land. To the east were a few large ranches owned by others as well as a large stretch of federal land comprising the west end of Gila National Park.

They drove in silence for fifteen minutes as the land grew sparser and the farm and pasture lands gave way to miles of open space.

"Haven't been out here in a while," Harley said. "Forgotten how pretty it is."

"Yup. Prettiest valley in the Southwest."

"And we're still lookin' at Morgan land, aren't we?" he said, pointing westward.

"Yup."

A few minutes later, Ben Morgan turned off the highway, taking a dirt road west. They rumbled along the rutted road for a mile or so before driving into an open area, green and verdant like the rest of Saguaro Valley. Thanks to an orographic effect, cloud formation and with it lots of moisture had created this lush, verdant valley surrounded by mountains with desert on the far sides to the east, west, north, and south. A handful of enormous ranches, including Morgan's Run, the Dillons', and a few smaller ones, made up much of the largely undeveloped valley. Three thousand year-round residents and an equal number of snowbirds, tourists, and wealthy vacationers delighted in its beauty and abundance. Over the years, the Valley's wealthiest residents had bought up most of the land, then deeded it back to conservancy groups with the understanding that they could farm it, but that it could never be developed.

What was unusual about the land in front of them was the miles and miles of mowed grass. Harley stared openmouthed. "Wow, I thought this was conservancy land?"

"Nope. I held this parcel out figuring it'd eventually go that route unless I decided to develop it."

"Develop it?" Harley asked, shock registering in his green eyes.

"Let's eat," the elder Morgan said, switching off the ignition. "You get Carmela's basket. Got a couple of camp seats and a fold-up table back there, too."

Ben grabbed the table and Harley the rest, following the man who was the nearest thing to a father he had. His own father had run off when Harley was four. He barely remembered him, a shadowy figure lurking around the edges of his young life. The memories were not pleasant. His mother had supported them through her job as housekeeper at the Lodge at Morgan's Run. Milly Langdon died during his first year of college, leaving him and his sister, Carrie, a ramshackle house on the outskirts of town, which they sold. When he came back after college, he lived at the ranch for a short time before buying his condo by the river. Carrie lived in

Wyoming with her husband, Corkie, and two kids. Corkie was a carpenter and Carrie made jewelry. Last he'd heard, they had joined a commune.

His boss led the way to the top of a rise, affording a beautiful view of the flat land and rolling hills. They set up the table and chairs and settled beside each other. "You developing a golf course?" Harley asked, as Ben rummaged in the picnic basket, pulling out sandwiches, cans of beer, iced tea, and lemonade, and enough food to feed ten.

Ben laughed, handing him a turkey sandwich stuffed with avocado, lettuce, and tomato. "Somethin' like that."

"I can't believe it. How long have you been clearin' this place?"

"Six months."

"Funny Ben never mentioned it."

"Doesn't know about it. Nobody does, not even Leonora."

"You mean to tell me crews have been working out here for six months and no one on the ranch has gotten wind of it?"

"Yup." Ben grinned, then took a bite of his sandwich. "Our Carmela is a darn good cook, isn't she?"

"How did you pull this off and why are you telling me? What the hell've you got goin' on here, Ben?"

"It's a joint venture, Spark and me. He brought the grading crew from Portland. They're livin' in Wilbur, so they don't get up to Saguaro. All the equipment and sod has been comin' from Prescott. As for the what is it, that depends on you, son."

"Excuse me?"

"Spark and I want to raise and train thoroughbred race horses. We've got feelers out for mares and stallions right now."

"You're kidding."

"Nope. We've been talkin' about this since our college days. Kind of the dream that never died. We both keep up with the circuit and when he moved down from Portland, we decided it's now or never."

Harley pushed his Stetson back, shaking his head. "Well, if you two don't beat all."

"We need you, son. We can't do this without you. I would've told you sooner, but we wanted to get the clearing done before we told anyone. It's gonna be a bang-up surprise."

"That's for sure."

"I wouldn't be spillin' the beans now if you weren't thinkin' of leavin' us. We never imagined this place without you at the helm. I can't think of another wrangler west of the Rockies who could take this on."

"What about your own sons?"

"I love our boys more than life itself, but there's not a one of 'em that could take this on."

"I don't know, Ben. I've accepted the Hayworth position. The contracts are coming today or tomorrow."

His boss nodded. "And you're a man of your word. I know that, son. It's one of the things I admire most about you. I'd guess we won't be ready for occupancy—beast or human—for six months to a year. We'd like you in on the planning stages, but we're flexible. If this is something you're interested in—and we darn well hope you are—we'll work around your timetable, even if it means you goin' to California till they find someone to replace you. You can still advise us long distance, and don't forget, we've got Spark's jet at our disposal whenever we need it."

"Ben, I don't know what to say."

"I'd be grateful if you'd say 'I'll think about it,' rather than flat-out refusing. We'll double what they offering you at Hayworth, or more, if that's what it takes. There's going to be a house for you, and houses for the head trainer and horse manager, and bunkhouses, cabins, you name it, for any employee who needs housing."

"You know Maggie or Jeb could do this."

"And I expect they'll help out from time to time, but they've got other fish to fry with the camp, schools, and the kids. They're good, son, but they aren't Harley Langdon or Ned Williams."

Harley laughed at the reference to Maggie's dad, the most famous wrangler the region had ever produced. "I'm hardly in Ned's class."

These days, his wrangling days behind him, Ned Williams took care of most of the Valley's livestock. Years earlier, he had completed most of his veterinary training, but had dropped out shortly before he could complete his degree so he consulted with vets in Tucson or Phoenix when needed.

"No time to be modest, son. You're up there and I know Ned would agree with me. I'm gonna push hard for him to come down here, too. What'dya say?"

Harley gazed down the valley, green and pristine as far as the eye could see. His boss was offering him the world, a dream job. A job that meant that he could stay in the Valley, living near the people he loved, including Willow. "I'll think about it, Ben. I really will."

Ben clapped his shoulder. "Whoopee! Wait'll I tell Spark!"

"What about the others? When are you going to tell them?"

"I'd like to keep this a secret, if we can. Depending upon your decision, I'd like bring Ned in before too long, but keep the others in the dark for a bit, at least till after the wedding."

"So I'll be public enemy number one with the Morgan clan no matter what I decide?"

The older man smiled. "Don't worry about them. I'll put in a good word for you, son. They'll calm down eventually."

Yeah, right, Harley thought, taking a long sip of Carmela's excellent iced tea. *And I'm Santa Claus.*

Chapter 6

After several hours of furious strawberry picking, Ruthie Morgan plopped down in the dusty path beside her overflowing basket and burst into tears. Beth, her sister, spied her as she headed toward the farm's small office building.

"Hey, Ruthie! It's lunchtime! Come on in!"

When Ruthie didn't budge, Beth walked out to meet her just as Jo Jo, one of the pickers, came to collect the basket brimming with strawberries.

"Thanks, Jo Jo," Beth said, as the man withdrew. She reached out her hand. "Come on, sweetie. Let's eat. You'll feel better." Their brother Robbie had told her about Harley's defection an hour earlier, so Beth was not surprised to find her sister in such a state.

Ruthie gazed up, her dirt-smudged face streaked with tears. "I'll never feel better again."

"Don't be silly."

"You don't understand! I've loved him as long as I can remember."

"With many boyfriends along the way."

"None of them meant anything! I just wanted to make him jealous, and let him know I was old enough to fall in love."

"What about your engagement?"

"That, too. When Kev asked, I figured, why not? I'd waited long enough. Then Harley has to go and save my life! He opened up, you know, for a couple of minutes."

"I'm sure he was scared to death."

"Not scared enough to do anything about it."

Beth pulled her to her feet. "You know Harley. He's always been a man of few words."

"Well, he seems to have found enough words to take the job in Napa!"

Beth patted her shoulder. "To us he's just Harley, but he's pretty well-known outside the Valley. It's a huge step up for him, and besides, you never know what the future will bring, sweetie."

"Well, I know *his* future won't include me if we're eight hundred miles apart!"

They walked arm in arm to the back porch behind the farm office. Beth pulled their lunches out of the fridge and came to sit beside her and they ate in silence for several minutes. Finally, Ruthie looked over at her. "Do you think he loves me?"

Beth hesitated. *If I say 'yes' she'll get even more worked up, but if I lie it will break her heart.* Truth won out. "Yes."

"Then why won't he tell me?"

Beth patted her knee. "I don't know, sweetie. Only Harley can answer that."

Tired of a subject that did nothing but tie her in knots, Ruthie said, "Aunt Helen arrives today."

"Great! So she'll be at dinner, then? It'll be fun for Mother to have her. I hope someday she'll bring the rest of the family. All those cousins we've never met." Helen had four daughters, all of whom lived in New England. Only one, Lucy, the eldest, was married with children.

Ruthie sniffed, another tear trickling down her dirty cheek. "When I think about all Aunt Helen's been through in her life, I feel like a big baby. But I love him, you know? I don't know how to love anyone else."

"One day at a time, sweetie. How's the picking going? You want to take off early? I could call Lang. I'm sure he can relieve the sitter and you and I can grab a drink at the Bulldog before we head home. That is, if you wash your face beforehand."

"Thanks, sis. Let's see how the afternoon goes. There'll be plenty to drink tonight and I intend to have at least a gallon of Raoul's margaritas!"

"That's the spirit!" Beth said. "I gotta get over the washing shed to start on the strawberries and get ready for the mountains of spinach you're bringing in, right?"

"Absolutely. I'll head out now and see how the guys are doing. Thanks, Bethie."

"No problem," her sister said, thinking about the explosive evening ahead of them. *Between Ruthie and my hot-headed older brother, Harley Langdon would be smart to feign illness and stay home!*

***

When he returned to the stables after lunch, Harley breathed a sigh of relief that his best friend's Rover was not parked beside the barn. He had left Ben's dad with the promise to think about his offer. He checked the message board and found that Jeb and Nick were still out on the trails with two of their more experienced riders. He considered saddling Pepper, his Appaloosa, and riding out to join them, but duty called. He began making lists for the pack trip and spent an hour in the office, calling suppliers.

He was just heading out to check the corrals when Jeb and Nick rode up with their clients, Pat Wordell and Liz Baron. Both the women were wives of ranch owners who preferred to board their horses here rather than their own stables. This oddity was almost entirely due to the presence of Harley Langdon, with whom they were both in love.

Harley grinned, tipping his hat. "Ladies, good ride?"

Liz flipped her hair back. "The best, though we missed you, cowboy." Liz was what one would call a handsome woman, tall, big-boned, and buxom. Her husband, Roger Baron, ran the only dairy farm in the Valley. The milk, cream, cheese, and yoghurt from his prized Lincoln Reds were sought after by specialty markets and restaurants throughout the Southwest.

The Wordell family raised turkeys. Pat's husband, Paul, came from a wealthy Phoenix family, so the turkeys were more of a hobby. She was a petite blonde with turned-up nose and skin-tight jeans. "Thanks, Nicky," she said as she slid off her tall Arabian, into his arms.

Parker smiled, setting her down. "My pleasure, Ms. Wordell."

"Oh, you naughty boy! I told you to call me Patty!"

"Shall I take her in?" he asked, indicating the beautiful horse beside her.

"Thanks, hon. Gotta run."

"Me, too, sweetie," Liz said, handing the reins of her American paint horse to Jeb. "Thanks for an incredible ride, sweetie. You're gonna have to bring that boy of yours over to watch the cows come in." As she passed Harley, she pointed. "Next time, you're taking us out, mister. No excuses!"

As the ladies disappeared, Parker gave him a mock bow. "Harley, darlin', what'cha want us to do after we groom these two?"

"Watch it, Parker, unless you want to be out of a job. How'd it go out there? Were the trails clear after the storm?"

"Pretty good," Jeb said.

"Where's Maggie?"

"She went down to camp about an hour ago." As he spoke, Jeb gazed toward the far side of the barn, spying Ben Morgan's Rover screech to a stop. "Uh-oh. Come on, Nick. Let's get these horses cooled down."

"Shit," Harley muttered, deciding he would check on Pepper grazing in the far corral. As he walked, he considered what he should or could say to the man who, with only a few exceptions, knew his every secret. *Maybe he'll be in such a rage that he won't notice I'm lying through my teeth?*

"Stop right there, Langdon!"

Here goes nothing. Harley turned to face his lifelong friend. Hands on hips, he watched Ben approach, wondering if he was about to get punched in the nose. "So you heard?"

"Damn right I heard, you bastard. What I want to know is, why didn't I hear it from you instead of my wife? She's devastated, you know."

"That's not how she appeared to me," he said calmly, knowing that no matter what he said it would be wrong.

"Well, she wouldn't, would she, for Christ's sake? Maggie's a saint. She'd never rain on your parade. How long have you been planning all this behind all our backs?"

Ben's face was beet red and Harley wondered if he should remind him about his finicky heart. Instead, he said, "Look, do you want to talk about this or just yell and cuss at me?"

"Fuck you, Langdon," he said, leaning against the corral fence, petting Rowdy, his sorrel quarter horse.

Pepper nudged alongside the slightly smaller horse. "I'm sorry, man. I was gonna tell you. It's all happened fast. Just found out and only told your dad yesterday. I mean, he's known about the possibility for a while. They did contact him, too. I wasn't lookin' for this, buddy, but it's kinda fallen in my lap."

"Yeah, right."

"After I was at Reagan Ranch, the manager gave Hayworth my name. He called, we talked, and Hayworth himself came down for lunch last week when you, Maggie, and the kids were away. I didn't think anything would come of it, you know?"

Ben shrugged.

"It's a lot more money, and I have Willow to think about. Talia's been pretty good lately, but they haven't given her much time."

Willow's mom was dying of breast cancer. A brief fling with Harley their freshman year at the University of Arizona had left her pregnant, and Talia had kept their daughter's existence a secret from him until recently.

"Don't pull that crap, buddy boy. I've seen your bank accounts. You're loaded." Ben was right. Harley lived frugally, saved every penny, and had invested wisely.

"College costs a fortune."

The fight knocked out of him, Ben took a deep breath. "So you're really leavin' us, huh?"

"Not for a while. Not till you find a replacement. Maybe months."

"And maybe we won't look very hard," Ben said, stepping back, a slight grin on his face.

"You know, buddy, you deserted this ship long before I did. First Stanford, then Santa Barbara. If it weren't for Maggie and Emma, you'd still be out there enjoying the high life."

Ben shrugged. "I'd have come to my senses eventually."

"If you had any."

"Maggie's already talking about coming to visit. They better build you a huge place out there 'cause it's gonna be our vacation destination. At least twice a year."

"Fine by me."

"You bringing Willow with you?"

"Not until something happens to Talia. Then I'll decide with her grandparents. She'll be in college in two years anyway."

"I don't envy you, buddy. Does your redheaded girlfriend know?"

"If you're referring to your little sister, yes, she knows and has already bitten my head off."

"Gonna be a fun dinner tonight. Lucky our aunt's visiting so people—and I mean Morgan people—will be on their good behavior."

"Be good to see Helen. She's a nice lady."

"That is, if you live long enough to say hello."

Harley laughed. "I'm gonna miss you, buddy."

"Same here. We'll just have to hire you back for regular consulting work."

The two men walked back to the barn and found Jeb and Nick just beginning to feed the horses.

CHAPTER 7

It was a warm summer evening as guests began to arrive at the Big House. Two long farm tables were set with Leonora's pottery, blue glassware, and beautiful linens, a riot of color on the wide stone terrace ringed by green lawns and gardens. Robbie and Raoul manned the bar and grill, and Aria Fiorelli, Spark Foster's chef, assisted Carmela in passing appetizers. Polly Granger and Lynn Manguilli, the newly hired teachers for the Cottage Day Care, had come early and were also assisting.

"We did a great job finding those two," Leonora said, watching Polly and Lynn talking with Carmela. "Lynn may the craziest dresser I've ever seen, but she's so capable. For a big woman, she is quite attractive."

"Yes, she is," her husband said, "and smart as a whip. She's gonna be great for Emma and Toby."

At twenty-seven, Lynn, the special educator and occupational therapist, was slightly older than Polly. A tall, heavy-set brunette with arresting charcoal eyes, she had a hearty laugh, and bohemian taste in clothes. Tonight she wore what appeared to be black capri-length yoga pants and a flowing peasant blouse, the fabric a pale green floral. Polly, an early childhood teacher, was Lynn's polar opposite. Thin, with straight blond hair, blue eyes, and freckles, she was dressed in khakis and a white tee shirt.

Helen Winthrop stood with her cousin and Ben Morgan Senior, greeting people as they arrived. A year younger than her cousin, Helen was tall and lean with pale blue eyes. She wore her thick salt-and-pepper hair in a long braid down her back. Tonight she was dressed in a long, flowing skirt, sandals, and a sleeveless white blouse and a colorful beaded necklace. Turning to her hosts, she said, "I am so impressed that you're building a day care on the ranch. I can't wait to see the Cottage."

Leonora patted her arm. "You'll have the full tour tomorrow. I'm so glad you're here."

"Me, too," Helen said. As Ben and his family tumbled in, the children running this way and that after the farm dogs, she added, "Thanks so much for having me. Just what I needed. To be surrounded by loving family."

"It's our pleasure, darlin'," Ben Senior said, his arm circling her shoulder. "Nora and I wish you'd stay permanently."

Leonora smiled at her. "Ben wants everyone he loves to stay and live on Morgan's Run and I couldn't agree more. We're thrilled to have you as long as you want to stay. Our kids have mostly flown the coop except Ruthie, and Robbie, but he's only here temporarily until he and Hope move into their place in town."

Helen smiled. "What's that expression about guests and old fish?"

"Nonsense. Here's our dear friend, Spark Foster. Hello, darlin'. I don't believe you've met my cousin Helen?" Leonora hugged her husband's buddy.

Helen held out her hand to the tall, handsome stranger, balding, tan, and fit. According to Leonora, Spark was often mistaken for the actor and politician Fred Thompson, and she could see why. In her opinion, he was a handsomer version. "Hello. I've heard so much about you, Mr. Foster."

"And I, you, although Ben and Nora forgot to mention your great beauty Ms. Winthrop." *And, she is a beauty, a lithe, mature beauty.* He bowed slightly.

For a second Helen thought he might kiss her hand. "Helen, please."

"And it's Spark, darlin'. No Mr. Fosters here."

Ben Morgan watched his friend. He'd forgotten what an inveterate flirt his college roommate could be. He hadn't seen Spark turn on the charm like this since he was dating Patsy, his beloved wife. After a long battle with cancer, Patsy had died several years earlier, leaving her devoted husband devastated.

"So sorry Amy and Jeb can't be here," Leonora said. "Emma and little Bennie will miss Toby."

"Gotta give the other grandparents a chance. Jake and Lily are as crazy about him as I am, doncha know," Spark said, referring to Jeb's parents, who lived in Flagstaff.

"Are they up north for the weekend or longer?" she asked.

"Till tomorrow. Then Jake and Lily are comin' down for the opening of camp and stayin' through the wedding. A kind of mini-vacation at Club Foster."

"Oh, how lovely," Leonora said. "Give you a chance to fill up that big house of yours. Now Spark, be a dear and escort Helen to the bar and get her a drink. Ben, will you get me a white wine, sweetie? I'm going to locate our youngest, who's no doubt pouting in her room."

"Too bad about Langdon," Spark whispered, exchanging a conspiratorial look with Ben Senior. *We're goin' straight to hell for this sneakin' around*, he thought, as he extended his arm. "Helen, shall we?"

"Well, who'd a thought," Ben Senior said, arm around his wife as they watched Spark and Helen cross the terrace.

"Me, that's who. Why do you think I asked her out here? I knew she and Spark would be perfect for each other."

"Did not!"

"Well, I had hopes," she said, smiling. "Now to find our baby. I hope I won't find her curled up in a ball with red puffy eyes!"

"She looked pretty good when I saw her a few minutes ago," he said.

"Speak of the devil," she said as Ruthie waltzed onto the terrace wearing a white sundress with bold pink and black flowers. It appeared to have been sprayed on and flattered every inch of her compact, curvaceous body. Its plunging neckline left little to the imagination, and her black strappy sandals with five-inch heels meant that she towered over her petite mother. Her flaming red hair fell loosely over her shoulders and huge silver hoop earrings dangled from her ears.

"Ruthie Ann, wherever did you get that dress? And those earrings! You look like a gypsy!"

"Gabriela's. You like it?"

"Yes…well, it's… No, of course I don't like it! Very inappropriate. Now go and change immediately!"

Ben Senior grinned from ear to ear. *That dress'll give Harley Langdon somethin' to think about!* "Leave her be, darlin'. I think she looks terrific."

"Well, you would!"

"Listen, Momma, you can just keep your snooty Cowbelle judgments to yourself. If every other woman in this family can shop at Gabriela's, so can I."

"Well, I've never seen anything like that come out of Gabriela's!"

"Well, now you have! She ordered it especially for me, thank you very much!"

As Ruthie sashayed toward the bar, Lang, Beth, and Lily came around the corner of the terrace and waved. "Thank goodness, sane people!" Leonora said, rushing to greet them.

"Hey, guys, welcome!" Ben Senior said, spying Harley stepping out of the house with Nick Parker. "You know guys where the bar is." He patted Harley's shoulder as they passed by, then headed over to greet Beth, Lang, and his newest grandchild.

"Wow, who the hell is that?" Parker asked, whistling as they strolled across the terrace.

"I believe it's the youngest Morgan," Harley said, bracing for the encounter. *Wow doesn't begin to cover it. I'd know that ass anywhere.*

CHAPTER 8

As they reached the bar, Ruthie turned. "Hey, Nick," she said, ignoring his companion. "The margaritas are delicious."

"Thanks, but I'll stick to beer."

"Chicken," she said, leaning toward him, giving him a lascivious grin.

"You look amazing," Nick said, "but I suspect you already know that."

"Thanks." With a flip of her hair, she turned and headed for the lawn, where Ben Senior was now playing with Emma and baby Ben.

Harley smiled, watching her ditch the five-inch heels as soon as she reached the grass. *Gonna to be a challenge roughhousing in that dress! Parker is right, though. She does look amazing.* The sight of her sent his libido into overdrive. *This is the little girl I've been putting off all these years? What am I, crazy?*

His best friend handed him a beer. "Better watch it, buddy. You're givin' yourself away with that look."

"What look?"

"The 'I wanta eat her whole' look."

"Where'd she get that dress?"

"Who knows. Give her ten minutes. It'll be covered with grass stains and mud."

"She is beautiful."

Ben poked him. "Hey, man, pull yourself together."

"I mean it."

"I know you do, 'cause you're as crazy in love with her as she is with you."

Harley shrugged. "She's better off without me."

"That's bullshit and you know it. Did you meet my mom's cousin Helen? Come on, I'll bring you over. Take your mind off your red-haired siren."

As Ben and Harley chatted with Helen and Spark, Leonora clapped her hands. "Dinner is served! Everyone grab a plate and head to the buffet!"

CHAPTER 9

In deference to her cousin, Leonora had asked Carmela to prepare an almost entirely vegetarian Southwestern meal, with the exception of the racks of ribs Raoul had grilled. There were tureens of butternut squash chipotle chili with avocado, sweet potato burritos smothered in avocado salsa verde, fried avocado tacos, grilled portobellos with her special sauce, elote grilled Mexican corn, enchiladas verde, and bowls of colorful salads at each table.

Still squiring Helen Winthrop about, Spark said, "You're in for a treat. Ben and Leonora have the best cook in the Southwest." He leaned closer and whispered, "But don't tell Aria I said that."

"Does she work here also?"

"No, she's my chef. She's helping out tonight. Gets bored when there's no one at home to cook for. Brought her with me from Portland."

"Lucky you," she said, smiling at him. She liked this tall, handsome cowboy, the first man to whom she'd been attracted since her second husband's death.

As everyone filled their plates from both sides of the buffet, Ruthie tried to attach herself to Nick Parker, but she had competition. Spark's chef was all over him every time she passed by. Finally, Ruthie wedged herself between Aria and Nick, a smug smile on her face. The raven-haired chef shrugged and turned her attention to Harley, who had been quietly observing the spectacle. That is, when he could tear his eyes away from "the dress" and more specifically the glorious body inside it. Her full, rounded breasts, usually strapped under a sports bra, were unleashed tonight. As she bent over a tray of enchiladas, he was afraid they might tumble into the guacamole. He felt himself growing hard and realized it had been a while since he'd been with a woman, never mind one who had stolen his heart when she was in pigtails.

"Come sit with Mags, the kids, and me," Ben said, watching his friend watch his baby sister. "Hopefully the redheaded bombshell will be seated elsewhere."

The elder Morgans, Spark, and Helen made their way to the longer table and beckoned to Lynn and Polly to join them as well as Lang and Beth. Lily was in a seat attached to the table, already covered with guacamole and mashed banana. Robbie joined them, taking a seat beside his niece, making funny faces at her.

"Where's your fiancée tonight?" Spark asked.

"She's down in Tintown. She's been packing up the studio and shop," Robbie said. "She'll be back with a U-Haul next week."

"You two taking up residence on the ranch?"

"Actually, we've rented an apartment in town. Condo. Same complex as Harley and Polly and Lynn."

"Yes," Lynn said, "we're neighbors."

"It's a pretty nice complex, and our unit faces the river," Robbie said. "Seemed like the easiest thing to do till we figure out where we're gonna live and what the heck I'm gonna do. I just wrapped things up in Sedona a few weeks ago, so neither of us has had a second to think things through."

"Plenty of time for that," his father said, winking at Spark. "We're hopin' they'll settle here and take one of the northwest parcels," his father said. "But it's their choice."

"Course it is. Uh-oh, I think I see trouble brewing at table two," Spark said, as they all observed Harley slip into an empty chair right next to Ruthie.

Leonora sighed. "Oh, Lord, that girl is gonna be the death of me. Helen, I don't know how you do it with four girls!"

Her cousin laughed. "We've had our moments."

*****

"This seat taken?" Harley asked softly, knowing damn well it wasn't. He had waited until everyone else was seated.

"Suit yourself," she said, turning up her nose and turning toward Emma, who sat on her other side.

Piqued that Aria had managed to maneuver Nick Parker to a seat opposite her, she now gave her full attention to her niece, who was startled by her aunt's sudden barrage of questions and silly remarks.

"It's gonna be a long meal," Maggie whispered to Ben as she attempted to feed baby Ben a slice of portobello mushroom. Just like his dad, portobellos were one of his favorite foods.

"Watch Langdon. That dress has him completely unhinged."

She smiled at her husband. "It's about time."

"Harley," Aria drawled, leaning over the table. "I'd really like to start riding regularly. Would you be free to give me some private lessons?"

"Not unless you're planning to drive to Napa for your lesson," Ruthie snapped. "Haven't you heard? He's deserting us!"

"No, really? That's too bad," Aria said, the only person at the table surprised by Ruthie's announcement.

"Guilty as charged, but not deserting. Just trying something new."

As Harley launched into a description of the Hayworth Ranch and their programs, Maggie listened to her boss, shocked to find him so loquacious. If anyone could get more than a sentence out of the taciturn cowboy, they were lucky. At that moment, baby Ben threw a handful of rice at his sister, who screamed, "Stop it!"

As the table's attention turned to the antics of the children, Ruthie took a deep breath, every fiber of her being acutely aware of the man beside her. Every time his arm brushed against her, heat radiated through her.

"You look beautiful," he said softly.

So surprised she nearly dropped her taco in her lap, she said, "Fine time to be nice to me."

"I'm just telling it like it is."

"Well, don't!"

He reached under the table and took hold of her hand. She gasped and her face turned bright red. The interplay was not lost on their tablemates, but by tacit agreement, they endeavored to ignore the pair, holding their breath.

Harley stroked her callused palm with his thumb.

For a brief moment, Ruthie gave in and returned his touch. Then, without warning, she yanked her hand away and for the rest of the meal kept both hands on the table. When the desserts were served, Harley excused himself and said good-night to his hosts, passing a buffet table now filled with plates of cookies, slices of tres leches cake, churros with coconut sauce, and bowls of homemade ice cream.

"Poor guy," Ben said, watching his friend's retreat. "He'll never be the same after seeing her in that dress."

Maggie laughed. "I think you may be right. She does look pretty, though, doesn't she? Not our little Ruthie anymore."

"You're tellin' me. We're gonna have to guard her like hawks when Harley leaves. Every bozo in the Valley'll be sniffin' around her."

Maggie laughed, patting his shoulder. "News flash, big brother, that's been happening for quite some time now. You and your best bud are the only obtuse ones who haven't noticed."

CHAPTER 10

Ruthie woke at five a.m. with a terrible headache after too many margaritas. She usually tried to get to the farm by seven thirty, so she had two and a half hours to kill. She smiled, gazing over at "the dress" hanging on her closet door. She pulled on jeans, a tee shirt, and boots and tiptoed down the stairs. No one was up, including Carmela. She grabbed a bagel and banana and slipped out the door.

When she arrived at the stables, the only vehicle parked next to the barn was Nick Parker's truck. "Darn," she muttered, hoping to have the stables to herself. She found him raking out Misty's stall as she passed through on the way to the tack room. She waved but did not stop to chat. After grabbing Jadie's tackle, she led her pinto out the rear doors. As she secured the saddle, Parker emerged. "Goin' somewhere?"

"Just felt like a ride before work. I might even ride Jadie up to the farm and she can graze there for the day."

"Alone?"

"She'll be fine," she replied, fully aware that he was not referring to her horse.

"Ranch rules. No one rides alone."

"That's only for guests. Doesn't apply to the family."

Nick stood in front of the horse, taking hold of her halter. "Look, I didn't make the rules, but my bosses say—"

"I am one of your bosses, in case you've forgotten. Now get the hell out of my way."

"Suit yourself, but I'm calling Maggie and Harley."

"You just do that. And I'll call my dad and you'll be fired before the day is out."

"Yeah, right, anything you say, Ms. Morgan," he said, dropping the halter and stepping aside. "Just don't break your neck out there."

Nick watched her mount the pinto in one easy leap. Jadie responded to her slight nudge and they galloped out of the yard in a cloud of dust. Then he headed for the office to find his cell phone. He called Harley first, but it went straight to voice mail, so he tried Maggie. Ben Morgan answered, "Mornin', this is Maggie Morgan's cell."

"Hey, Ben, it's me, Nick."

"What's up, buddy?"

"Your little sister just rode outta here on Jadie. She's mad as a hornet. When I tried to stop her going alone, she threatened to call your father and have me fired."

Ben shook his head. "Jesus, I'm getting sick of her friggin' tantrums. Don't call Harley, whatever you do. Ruthie'll be fine. She's a good rider. She's gotta get to work, so she won't go far."

"I know she's your sister, man, and I know the whole Harley thing's got her all shook up, but she was a real bitch. I know I'm just an underling, but I don't need that shit."

"I know, buddy. I'm really sorry. I'll make it up to you, I promise."

He hung up and found Maggie behind him, holding a half-dressed toddler. "Ben, what's wrong?"

"My spoiled brat of a sister, what else? She's apparently pulled rank on Parker when he tried to stop her from riding alone."

"Oh, dear. Where's Harley?"

"I dunno, but I hope he's planning on coming in late. Jesus Christ!"

***

Ruthie reined Jadie in as the trail veered westward out of sight of the stables. "Whoa, girl, that's it." She decided to ride the ranch loop and then maybe take one short side trail rather than climb into the foothills. Embarrassed at her interaction with Nick Parker, she resolved to apologize as soon as she returned. *How dare I treat him like that? What's wrong with me?* She blinked back tears. For a second, she considered turning back, then decided her apology could wait for the forty-five minutes it would take to complete the loop. *Maybe I could offer to take him to dinner sometime? He's a great guy who certainly did not deserve to be caught in the middle of my heartbroken temper tantrum.*

***

After speaking with Ben Morgan, Nick went back to the stalls. Rip and Sandy had arrived and were waiting for him. He had just finished outlining the day's chores when Harley came in, Maggie right behind him. "Shit," he muttered. He had hoped the spoiled brat would have returned before his bosses got in.

"Morning, guys," he called.

Maggie walked slightly behind Harley and shook her head, meaning *Don't say a thing.*

"Where are we?" Harley asked.

"Guys are all set. First lesson's at nine so I'll stay with them until then."

"I'll take the horses out," Maggie said. "Then I've got to check in at camp. I'll be back for Nancy Grady's lesson."

"I'll help with the horses. Then I've gotta call suppliers," Harley said.

"Go," Maggie said, waving her hand. "I can handle this. I know you have a lot to do with the—"

"Where's Jadie?" Harley asked.

Nick looked at Maggie.

Harley gazed from one to the other. "What the hell's goin' on?"

Maggie swallowed, turning to face him. "Ruthie has her. She'll be back soon."

"Who's with her?"

"No one. Sorry, boss," Nick said.

Maggie stepped between them. "Now, Harley, Nick didn't have a choice."

"Of course he didn't! That brat should be horsewhipped pulling a stunt like this after last winter." He referred to Ruthie's fall during a camping trip, a fall that had broken her leg and nearly killed her.

Hand on his arm, Maggie said, "Harley, wait. Let me go."

"What, so you can break your neck trying to save that spoiled brat!"

Pepper was saddled in lightning speed and Maggie and Nick stood side by side, shaking their heads as they watched him tear out of the yard.

He whistled. "She may have been a little bitch to me, but I wouldn't want to be in her shoes right now."

"Hmm," Maggie said, smiling. "You never know. It could work out."

Laughing, they began the day's work.

CHAPTER 11

Ruthie decided to take the Mesa Trail leading westward off the Ranch Loop for about a mile, the terrain a gradual rise to a small mesa about as wide as two tennis courts. It was one of the places she and her dad would go when she was just learning to ride. The mesa afforded an unobstructed view to the western mountain range on the other side of the Gila River. In truth, it was more of a butte due to its relatively small size. It was covered with grass in places, and loose rock and dirt in others. She slipped off Jadie and took out the bagel she had stuffed in her pocket. After one bite, she broke it into pieces and scattered them to the wind.

The horse nuzzled her chin, nickering softly. "Oh, Jadie, what a fool I've been. I've been chasing a dream my whole life, thinking a stupid, childish crush would ever amount to anything more."

After a few minutes, she hopped back in the saddle and they started down. *Time to face the music.* As they descended, she spied a rider on the Loop veering off and heading their way. *Geez, slow down, buddy,* she thought, then gasped as she recognized both rider and his huge horse. *Just when I thought this morning couldn't get any worse!*

As they met up, Jadie reared, always a little afraid of the much larger horse. "Hey, girl," she said, "it's okay."

"Come on, let's go," he said, his voice low and quiet.

She thrust out her chin, glaring at him. He looked incredibly handsome this morning, green eyes shaded under his familiar worn Stetson. Harley Langdon was the most gorgeous man she'd ever known. She had measured every other guy against his impossible standard and they always came up lacking. Strong, tanned hands held Pepper back so he wouldn't spook the pinto.

"I'm finishing the Loop."

Once again he marveled at the transformation in his friend's youngest sibling. It was as if she'd grown overnight from a gangly little girl into an amazing, beautiful, albeit exasperating, woman. "No, you're not. I've got work to do."

"Go back to the barn, Langdon. You are not my boss and I don't have to answer to you."

As she nudged Jadie forward, Harley leaped from his horse and grabbed the pinto's halter.

"Let go of her," Ruthie cried, trying to kick his hand free.

In answer, he grabbed her by the waist and pulled her from the horse and into his arms. Ruthie struggled, but he held fast, drawing her to him, lips finding hers. As his tongue parted her full, rosy lips, Ruthie found her legs buckling underneath her. To steady herself, she held on to his shoulders. For a few seconds she opened herself to him, her tongue finding his, responding.

Lost in a storm of feeling that took his breath away, Harley felt his erection grow as her hips pressed against him. All of a sudden, Pepper nudged him and he came to his senses, releasing her. He looked down to find her in a swoon, eyes closed. Smiling, he watched as opened her eyes.

Spying his wolfish grin, she pushed him away. "I hate you, Harley Langdon!"

"No, you don't, sugar."

"Don't you dare call me sugar!"

"Tasted pretty sugary to me."

"If you had a shred of decency, you'd apologize!"

"On the contrary, my dear, I enjoyed every second, and so did you."

"Did not! I hate you! Get away from me!"

She jumped on Jadie and rode off, heading south. Laughing, he mounted Pepper and followed her until they reached the cutoff to the farm. She paused, turning in the saddle until he caught up. When he drew up alongside her, she glared at him. "I'm taking Jadie to the farm for the day, so don't you dare follow me!"

"Don't you think you owe Parker an apology?"

"That's none of your goddamn business! Now why don't you go and pack your bags for California and leave me alone!"

She kicked Jadie's flanks and flew off in a cloud of dust. Harley watched her go, shaking his head. *An amazing rider, and amazing woman. To think the love of my life may have been right here under my nose all this time. Too late for us now, but that was one hell of a kiss!*

CHAPTER 12

Beth Morgan Dillon stood beside the washing shed as her sister rode up, her hair wild and flying behind her. Ruthie leaped from the saddle and handed Jadie to one of the men. "Can you take off her saddle and tack and put her in the east pasture for the day?" He nodded, and she turned away, stalking into the farm office building. She did not appear to have seen her sister.

Beth shook her head. *Here we go!* When she reached the office, Ruthie was slamming drawers, throwing papers, and pacing from desk to window.

"What happened?"

"Nothing!" She kicked the trash basket, which toppled over.

"Ruthie, that's enough! If you're this upset, go home and cool down. We have too much going on today to deal with this. If you can't work, I'll phone Robbie. I'm sure they can spare him."

Her sister stopped pacing and stood, staring out the window. "He just kissed me! Right there on the Loop Trail! How dare he just grab me like that."

"Isn't that what you've been waiting for all these years?"

"Not like this!"

"How did you two happen to be out there together anyway?"

Ruthie sat on a wobbly stool, head down, arms outstretched. "I felt like a ride, that's all. An early morning ride by myself to clear my head."

"And?"

"First Nick Parker tried to stop me with the stupid 'no riding alone' rule, and I was incredibly rude to him, which made me feel so ashamed. Then that loathsome cowboy comes riding out to rescue me like some kind of vigilante and when I told him to go away, he grabbed me off my horse and kissed me. How dare he?"

"What was it like?"

Ruthie looked up at her. "What do you think it was like? It was incredible, of course, which makes it all the more horrible!"

Beth laughed, handing her a tissue box. "Let's get to work. It'll take your mind off things."

Ruthie spent all morning picking what would likely be the last of the strawberries for a few months, plus several baskets of raspberries and herbs for the Saturday market. As noon approached, she realized she'd forgotten to bring lunch. She made the rounds, asking if anyone else wanted lunch, then phoned in an order to Gracie's Diner in town. She took a ranch truck and had just returned with the food when her father drove up.

"Hey, Dad, let me get these to the guys and I'll be right back."

Her father headed for the back porch of the office building, grabbed a bottle of water, and waited. When his youngest returned, she joined him.

"What's up?" Ruthie asked, sitting beside him. "Beth's out with Raoul and the guys, making decisions about Friday's slaughter."

"It's you I came to see, Ruthie Ann."

His daughter stared at him, for the first time noticing his expression. Her mother called her Ruthie Ann when she was cross, but she couldn't remember her dad ever calling her that. "Something wrong, Dad?"

"I'm here about this morning."

Reluctantly, she set her bag of food aside. "Who told you?"

"Does it matter?"

"Only if it was that turncoat."

"Harley didn't say a thing, but he has a perfect right to ban you from the stables, if he decides that's warranted."

"Not for long, he doesn't."

"Nick Parker is a valued employee. He is also a part of this family."

Ruthie put up her hands, "I know, I know, I treated him very badly and I intend to apologize."

"When?"

"This afternoon when I bring Jadie back."

"Well, I'm afraid that's just not good enough this time, darlin'. He deserves more and you're gonna give it to him. Tomorrow morning, Robbie'll head up here and you're doin' Parker's work until noon."

"What? That's crazy. Whose idea was that? Don't tell me. I already know. The self-righteous jerk. As if he hasn't lost his temper a jillion times over the years."

"Never to valued and valuable employees. Besides, it isn't Harley's idea. It's mine."

"How could you, Dad?"

"You are my dear daughter and I love you more than life itself, but this has got to stop. You are twenty-six years old and still acting like a spoiled, entitled child."

"Mom put you up to this, didn't she?"

"Your mother knows nothing about this and I would prefer that it stay that way. We have always been tremendously proud of *all* our offspring. We did not raise you to be rude or supercilious to anyone, especially our employees. This ranch is run as a family and you *will* respect every member."

Shocked to her core by her beloved parent's tone and words, she said, "I don't believe what I'm hearing."

"One more thing—Harley is leaving. It's his choice, but I fully support it. It's a wonderful opportunity and we should all be glad for him. I know you have deep feelings for him, but he's not going to Mars and he will stay in our lives one way or the other. Ben and Maggie are already talking about vacationing in Napa. You can, too."

"Yeah, right."

"So what's it going to be, darlin'?"

"What if I refuse?"

"I'm hoping you won't. I've asked very few things of you in your life, but I'm askin' now."

"Okay, Dad."

"Good. Now eat your lunch and get back to work. Produce doesn't pick itself." He rose, smiling at his youngest, as he held out his arms.

Ruthie fell into them, head on his shoulder stifling a sob. "It's just so hard, Dad."

"I know, baby, I know." As he turned to go, he said, "And by the way, no one knows about the Parker work thing but you and me. I'll leave it to you to arrange things with Robbie for tomorrow morning."

CHAPTER 13

Midafternoon, Ben Morgan returned to the stables after working at Emma's Dream helping to repair cabins and get the pool and recreation areas opened up and ready for the first wave of campers. Maggie went back and forth when she wasn't checking on Emma and baby Ben. This summer, they would have hired a nanny for their two children, but with the ranch day care nearly ready to open, they had hired a local woman, Sally Pruit, to watch the kids for a few weeks. Polly and Lynn had offered, but Maggie insisted they put their full attention into settling into their condo and organizing the Cottage.

Maggie poked her head into the office, where Ben and Harley were discussing logistics for the upcoming pack trip. "I'm headed home," she said. "Will you be long?"

"Ten minutes, sweetheart."

Maggie disappeared and Ben turned to his friend. "So, are we set, buddy?"

"Pretty much. About half the party will need orientation and probably a few lessons before we head out. Thank God they're coming early. I see ten days of hell."

Ben nodded. "It's a long time to be away, but Parker and Jeb can handle things here, and Robbie said he'll help out. Rip and Sandy do all the grunt work anyway."

"Yup."

"You doin' okay otherwise?"

"Yup."

"No regrets?"

"A few."

"Wanta talk about it?"

"Not now. Maybe later. Go home. Parker and I can close up."

"Adios," Ben said. As he stepped outside the barn and headed for his Rover, he caught sight of a lone rider coming down the road from the farm. *Oh, boy*, he thought, recognizing his sister. *Here we go again.*

"Hey, sis. This is a surprise."

"Yeah, right," she said, slipping off Jadie and leading her into the barn. "I'm sure you're heard an earful. Looks like you're leaving. Bye!"

He considered sticking around to referee, but decided he'd rather be with his family. "See ya," he said, as she disappeared into the barn.

After putting Jadie in her stall, Ruthie hastened through the barn to the back corrals. Nick was bringing in Raffles, one of the Friesians they had rescued and rehabilitated. Parker, who was already known in the Valley as a horse whisperer, had done the lion's share of the work with them, especially Raffles, the smaller of the two. At first, they had doubted the horribly mistreated horse would survive, but he had, in large part due to Nick. Gentle and kind, Raffles was already one of the stable's safest mounts for beginning riders.

When he spied Ruthie, Nick nodded. "Ms. Morgan, is Jadie back? I'll take care of her as soon as I get the others in."

"Thanks, but I'll feed and cool her down. I wanted to catch you first."

"I'm kind of busy."

"I know. What I have to say won't take a minute. Please, Nick?"

He stopped nuzzling Raffles and turned to her, hands on hips. "Okay."

"I want to apologize. I was completely out of line this morning. I was rude, childish, and incredibly disrespectful to you. I am not a snob, truly I'm not, but I sure acted like one, and a rich bitch, too. That's not me. I'm not asking you to forgive me, be my friend, or even tolerate me. I just wanted to apologize and tell you that

I will be here from six thirty to noon tomorrow to muck out the stalls and do any work you want to give me. You can sit in the shade and observe if you want to."

"That's not necessary."

"But it is. Please let me do this."

Her eyes pleaded, and for a second Nick thought she might burst into tears. "Well, if it means that much to you."

"It does. Thank you, Nick. I'll go take care of Jadie now!"

As Ruthie headed in, Harley ducked into the office and closed the door. He had been listening from the shadows just inside the barn door. *She's grown up in more ways than one,* he thought, suddenly ashamed of his eavesdropping. Once he was sure Ruthie was busy with Jadie, he headed out to help Nick bring in the horses.

When the last horse was settled, Nick grabbed his jacket from the office, "Night, boss." Going through a familiar evening ritual between man and horse, he stopped at Raffles's stall and spent a few minutes rubbing his nose, softly talking to him, before walking to his truck. "Night, Ruthie," he called as he passed by.

"See you in the morning," she said.

A few minutes later, she was cleaning up and saying her goodbyes to Jadie when Harley caught her at the stall door.

"Hey."

She jumped. "Oh, I thought everyone had gone."

"Sorry to startle you."

"I'll live," she said, afraid to look him in the eye.

As she turned to walk out, he grasped her arm. "Ruthie, wait."

"Please let go," she said, refusing to look at him as his heat coursed through her body. *In an earlier time, I'd have turned and jumped into his arms.*

"I'm sorry," he said softly. "I behaved like a horse's ass this morning, riding out like Wild Bill Hickok, ready to lasso you and bring you in."

"Yes, you did, but I deserved it. Now please let go. I'm really tired and I want to go home and shower."

"Ruthie?"

"What?" she said, half turning.

"I'm sorry if I've hurt you."

Every fiber of her being yearned for him. She took a deep breath and steeled herself, turning to face him. There was a warmth and peace in his eyes that she'd never seen. "I've been a stupid little fool. All these years of running after you when you had no interest whatsoever. I've ruined more relationships than I can count pining away for you. I feel like I've woken up from a long dream. I *finally* get it."

If you only knew how much I adore you, he thought, knowing that it would be unfair to profess love now that he might be jumping ship. "You're family, Ruthie Ann Morgan. That will never change."

She smiled. "That's the second time someone's called me Ruthie Ann today, never a good sign. I know we're family, and I'm glad of that," she said, grasping his forearm. "And I'll always be grateful that you are a part of my life."

Jesus, babe, you're killing me! "Well, have a good night."

"You too," she said, letting go and turning away. Faint with longing and loss, she felt as if her heart had been ripped from her chest.

Harley watched her go, rooted to the spot, unable to move. At that moment, he wanted her more than he'd ever wanted any woman, and now she was gone. Lost to him forever. He shook his head. *Talk about stupid fools!*

CHAPTER 14

"So, have we heard anything from Mr. Langdon?" Spark asked as he sat with Ben Senior on the terrace of the Big House.

"Not yet, but give him a few days. I'm prayin' he'll come around."

"What's our plan B?"

"Hell if I know!" his friend replied, and both men chuckled. "Never even considered we might need a plan B."

"Don't s'pose young Jeb or Parker could do it?"

"Too green," Ben said. "Besides, no tellin' what your son-in-law will decide after he finishes school."

"Whatever it is, it'll be in the Valley, what with them building their house and all."

"So they've decided to build, then?"

"Ninety percent certain," Spark said, "which is about as close as you can get with these young folks."

"I think I hear the ladies, so remember, mum's the word on plan A and B," Ben said as Leonora and Helen appeared.

"Hi, guys," Leonora said, giving her husband a peck on the cheek. Spark stood, and after hugging her, he gave Helen a warm embrace.

"I invited Spark for dinner," Ben said. "Carmela's got plenty."

"Always does. Let Helen and me get a drink and we'll join you."

"Sit, ladies," Spark said. "What's your pleasure?"

"White wine for me, dearie," Leonora said. "Helen?"

"That sounds perfect. Thanks, Spark."

As the four settled into conversation, Ruthie slammed in the front door. "Uh-oh," Leonora said. "Sounds like someone's had a rough day."

Ben waited fifteen minutes, then excused himself. "Can I freshen anyone's drink?"

"Why don't you bring out the bottle, darlin'?" Leonora said. "And ask Carmela when she thinks dinner will be ready."

"Will do." Eying their wineglasses, Ben realized he had a few minutes, so instead of heading for the kitchen, he took the stairs and knocked on Ruthie's door. She opened it fresh from the shower in a bathrobe, with wet hair.

"Sorry to bother you, sweetie. Got a few minutes for an old man?"

She stepped back and opened the door wider. "I'm fine, Dad. I apologized, Nick accepted my offer, and that's that."

"I know you're angry, honey."

"I'm not angry. I just don't want to talk about it anymore."

"Spark's here for dinner with your mom and Helen. Haven't seen Robbie yet, but he should be home soon. You joining us?"

"I don't think so."

"Oh?"

"I'm going into town with friends," she lied.

"Okay, I'll let Carmela know. Got a hug for your old man?" he asked, noticing the set of her shoulders.

She hugged him stiffly, then pulled back.

He looked down, eyes sad. Ben Morgan loved all his children, but he'd always had a soft spot for his youngest. They were incredibly close. Each knew the other's thoughts without speaking. His beloved child was hurting and angry and there was not a damn thing he could do about it. "Have fun, sweetie," he said, leaning forward and kissing the top of her head.

Ruthie waited until his steps receded, then called Robbie's cell. "Hey, sis, what's up?" he said.

"Where are you?"

"Havin' a beer with Lang and Beth. Why?"

"Wanta have dinner at Gracie's? Spark's here with Mom, Dad, and Helen. I was thinking of asking Polly and Lynn to meet us."

"Sure thing. Lemme come back and shower and I'll see you in a few."

Ruthie phoned Polly and Lynn, who agreed to meet them at Gracie's at seven. Satisfied that she had arranged an evening to take her mind off her disastrous day, Ruthie went down and had a drink with her elders.

CHAPTER 15

After dinner, Ruthie, Polly, Lynn, and Robbie walked down the street to the Daily Scoop. A warm summer night, they sat on benches near the town square enjoying their ice cream. As they chatted, Robbie gazed down the sidewalk. "Hey, buddy, come join us!" he called as his companions turned to spy Harley walking toward them.

"Hey," he said, nodding to all four, his eyes soft as they landed on Ruthie.

"What'dya up to?" Robbie asked.

"Just came from dinner at the Bulldog and thought I'd grab my one cone of the season."

A health nut, Harley rarely, if ever, ate junk food or sweets.

Or your last before you desert us, Ruthie thought. "They're really good," she said, smiling.

When Harley disappeared into the ice cream shop, Polly said, "He's sure a handsome guy. Is he married?"

Robbie laughed. "The elusive Mr. Langdon, the most eligible bachelor in the Valley? Hardly. If he dates, he keeps it top secret." Spying his sister's face, he regretted his words.

"Well, he's gorgeous, that's for sure," Lynn said, "but I like my guys a little meatier, like me."

Harley returned with a small chocolate cone and sat beside Ruthie. "Did you all eat in town?"

"Gracie's," Lynn said. "Best diner in the world."

Polly nodded. "We're gonna be best friends with Gracie and her staff in no time. Neither Lynn nor I is a very good cook."

"Then you'll eat often at the Big House or get invited to Spark's," Ruthie said. "Both Spark and my parents have amazing cooks." As she spoke she was acutely aware of him beside her. The brush of his arm on hers was electric.

"I'll say," Polly said. "Dinner the other night was beyond incredible."

"And typical," Harley said. "There's nothing like a Morgan spread." *Not sure how much longer I can sit beside you without ravaging you on the spot, Ruthie Morgan.*

The group chatted a while longer before Lynn and Polly said their good-nights. "We're up early," Lynn said. "Tomorrow's the day we move into the Cottage."

"Good luck," Robbie said. "Let us know if you need help."

"I believe your mom's got a whole crew coming."

"I'm sure she does," Ruthie said. "Don't let her bully you. When the heavy lifting's over, shoo her out so you can think. If you don't set boundaries now, Leonora will drive you insane."

Robbie nodded. "She's right. This is your ship. Don't let Mom take command. And if she does, Maggie, Amy, and Beth can help you. They're a strong threesome, and they're the moms in this venture."

"Thanks for the tips," Lynn said. "Night, everyone. Harley, we'll see you around the condos."

He tipped his hat. "Night, ladies."

Robbie's cell phone rang and he excused himself, walking a short distance down the street to talk.

"How you doin'?" Harley asked Ruthie.

"Same as I was two hours ago," she replied, afraid to say more.

Robbie came back immediately. "Listen guys, I gotta run. Hope's truck broke down just outside of town."

"Want help?" Harley asked.

"Thanks. Tow truck's on the way. I'm gonna meet her and unload her gear into my truck. Harl, can you drop Ruthie off?"

"Sure thing, buddy."

"But I can go and help," she said.

"No prob," Robbie said, turning and jogging toward his truck.

Maybe not for you, she thought, watching him disappear.

CHAPTER 16

Harley grinned, wondering if Robbie had thrown them together on purpose. "So, it's just you and me, babe."

"I'd better get going soon. I've got an early morning tomorrow."

"Okay, truck's at my place."

They strolled the three blocks in silence, darkness descending. As they neared his condo complex, she said, "Do you know that in all the years you've lived here, I've never been in your apartment?"

"Not much to see."

"Does anyone ever visit?"

"Your brother, and Willow. That's about it."

"And your girlfriends."

He grinned. "You curious? Wanta come up?"

She stared at him, hesitating, then surprised herself by saying, "Okay, but just for a minute. Might be my last chance since you're moving out soon."

"Okay," he said, smiling.

"When *are* you moving out?" she asked as they ascended the stairs.

"Not for a while. I own the place, so I'm lookin' for a renter." He touched her arm at the top of the stairs. "This way."

"I mean, when do you leave?"

"Not until we find a replacement. Month or two, I'd guess." He unlocked the door. "Here it is. Don't mind the boxes. I was starting to clear bookshelves and get rid of some junk."

Ruthie gazed around the open space, living room, dining room, and kitchen, tastefully furnished with a roughhewn, Southwestern-style tables and chairs. A deep leather sofa was scattered with colorful throw pillows and the artwork on the walls reflected the region. Landscapes and several abstracts in oranges, reds, and yellows surrounded them. He also had a number of bird and animal carvings on bookshelves and the mantel. Over the fireplace, there was a large painting of the valley. Ruthie walked toward it and was not surprised to find that the artist was Hope Seymour, her brother Robbie's fiancée.

"Did you commission this?"

He shook his head. "Bought it about five years ago. She had an exhibit in Tucson."

"You go to art exhibits?"

"They're investments, but I know what I like. I've got four of hers. That one," he said, pointing to a small still life in the dining area. "And a couple more in my bedroom."

"Can I see?"

He grinned. "Suit yourself. It's that way."

Passing by a room he used as an office and spare bedroom, she stepped into a large bedroom dominated by a king-size bed, neatly made, a beautiful quilt in greens, blues, and beiges covering it.

"The two over the bed are Hope's," he said, pointing to small exquisite landscapes.

"Did you know you'd be having company?"

"I'm neat."

"Why am I not surprised?"

"My housekeeper was here today."

Boxes lined the wall beside a large cherry dresser. Avoiding the bed, she went to the dresser and examined the photos. "Willow's getting so grown up, isn't she? She's beautiful. Is her mom that pretty?"

He nodded. "She was pretty before she got sick. Now she's luminous."

Surprised at his candor, she turned to study his face. "Do you still love her?"

He shook his head. "There's an affection because we both love Willow, but no. Not sure I ever did. That was a long time ago, when I was young and foolish."

She glanced at the other photos, grimacing when she spied the one of her on crutches. "Why did you pick that one?"

"My family. I like it."

"And the stupid girl who wasn't watching where she was going and fell off a cliff."

"I know it was his fault," he said, recalling his rage at her fiancé.

"Who told you?" she asked, gazing at him in surprise. She had purposely made up a story about the fall so Harley would not feel compelled to kill Kevin for panicking and spooking Jadie.

"No one. I know when you're lying." He watched her, thinking she had never looked so beautiful or so vulnerable.

"Do not."

"Always have, since you were in preschool."

"Ha, ha," she said, the words catching in her throat as she noticed the softness in his green eyes. "You love me, don't you?"

"You're part of my family. Of course."

She was trembling, clasping her hands together to hide her feelings. "Why haven't you ever said?"

"It's never been our time, babe."

"What about now?"

"Probably not."

"Why not?" She took a step closer to him, gazing up with wide eyes.

She has her father's blue eyes, that same sparkle and softness, he thought, standing very still, hands at his sides lest he make a false move they would both regret. Her nearness was literally driving him crazy and he realized the mistake he'd made thinking he could give her a quick tour of the condo and then be on their merry way. This was Ruthie—impetuous, infatuated Ruthie—and his treacherous libido, which now seemed to go into overdrive every time he saw her. "You better not come any closer, babe, or I can't answer for the consequences."

"Oh? And what would they be?" She placed a hand on his chest and felt his heart pounding through his pale blue work shirt. She looked up and found raw desire in the green eyes she loved so much.

Harley grasped hold of her hand. "Better not start something neither of us can stop, Ms. Morgan."

"Who says I want to stop?" she asked.

"Sweetheart, I'm trying to protect you."

"I don't want protection, I want you," she said, her other hand tracing a line along his jaw. "If you're leaving me and the Valley behind, don't you think I deserve something to remember you by?"

"And you think us having sex is it?"

"I know it is. Now kiss me, cowboy. I've waited a long time for this." She stood on tiptoes as he bent and captured her full, rosy mouth, his tongue delving deep, thirsty for her.

Ruthie sighed and gave herself to him, her arms drawing him closer as he lifted her from the ground. He reached down and grasped her full, perfect ass, then her thighs as he wrapped her legs around his waist. They leaned against the wall, their bodies swaying and coming together in a long overdue dance of lust. After settling her legs, his right hand traced the lines of her body to her full, round breast, the nipples already hard as his fingers teased through her tee shirt.

She could feel his erection tickling her stomach and he groaned as she rubbed her body up and down against him. "I've waited so long for you, cowboy. Take me. I'm yours."

"Oh, my God, babe," he said, voice husky as he gazed down at her.

His lips moved down her neck as she pulled her tee shirt over her head, revealing a lacy white bra. He reached around and unclasped the strap, releasing her. His eyes traveled down to glimpse her glorious breasts for the first time, even more spectacular than he had imagined. "You have grown up, haven't you?" he said as he lifted her and captured one breast, then the other, his tongue circling each nipple, gently squeezing and nipping as Ruthie cried out, delirious.

"Oh, oh, oh!"

"This is only the beginning, babe. You asked for it and I'm gonna give it to you," he said, carrying her to the bed, laying her down and relieving her of her boots, socks, and jeans in what seemed like one fluid motion. As he slipped each garment off, his lips moved up and down her body. His tongue was everywhere as he inched her panties down, first fingers and then lips and tongue moving between her legs, licking, sucking, and finding her sweet core, bringing her to a crashing orgasm.

"Oh, Harley, oh, Harley, oh, oh, oh!" she cried, hands reaching down to him as he stayed just out of reach.

As the climax passed and she lay spent on the quilt, she gazed up to find him still fully dressed. "Not fair," she said, sitting up, coming closer, unbuttoning his shirt, and slipping it off his broad, muscular shoulders. She had seen him bare-chested many times over the years, his wiry, hard body a wonder to her and every other woman with eyes, but tonight she marveled at his sinewy chest now slick with sweat. She looked down to spy the huge bulge in his jeans and began stroking him, softly at first, then more insistently.

"Now I know you're trying to kill me," he said, leaning down to kiss her.

"You're damn right," she said, grasping hold of the top button of his jeans, fingers swiftly moving downward until she unleashed a part of his anatomy she had never seen before. The sight of his penis took her breath away as she grasped hold and began stroking, first with her hands, then wiggling around so she could take him into her mouth, her lips and tongue driving him insane.

"Don't know how long I can hold on, babe," he said huskily.

"Then don't," she said, straightening up and releasing him. "I've waited for fifteen years to feel you inside me, Harley Langdon, and I don't want to wait another instant." With that, she lay back on the bed, opened her legs, and smiled up at him.

"Oh, baby, here I come," he said, leaning over her as he guided himself into her warm, sweet depths with a thrust that filled her completely.

Ruthie wrapped her legs around him, meeting his every thrust as their wild, unbridled desire for one another finally found release. Only after they brought each other to a simultaneous, blinding climax and were lying wet and slick in each other's arms did he remember the condoms in his bedside table. *Shit, what the hell have you done, Langdon? This is what long-suppressed desire does. Makes you stupid!*

Ruthie head was in the crook of his shoulder and he nuzzled her, kissing her softly. "Hey, sweetie. That was incredible."

"Mmm," she murmured, kissing him, loving the feel of him inside her. She began to move her hips from side to side, stroking and squeezing him deep.

"Hey, babe, what about birth control? You using any?"

"We're fine," she said, moving more insistently.

"Sweetheart, I have condoms right here."

"Come here, cowboy. I said we're fine." Her eyes were closed and her body held his erection, her tightness and sweet lubricant astounding him.

Putting worry aside, his desire blinding him, Harley thrust deeper, his lips finding hers as they resumed their dance, more slowly this time, their orgasms undulating waves of sensation that seemed to last forever.

They fell asleep in each other's arms, and when they woke it was light out. Ruthie popped her head up, "What time is it?"

Harley smiled, kissing her nose. "Early."

"I promised Nick I'd be at the barn by six thirty."

"Well, it's barely five now, so come here." He drew her closer, pressing her round softness against him, his erection almost immediate. This time their lovemaking was sweet and slow. Afterward, she kissed him deeply, then drew back. "I'm sorry. I could stay like this forever, but I've got to go. Can I take a shower?"

"Help yourself," he said, indicating the bathroom door. His desire skyrocketed as he watched her beautiful nakedness as she crossed the room.

She had just stepped into the warm shower when she felt a draft and knew he'd joined her.

"Hello," she said, turning to face him.

Harley gazed down, kissing her. "Let me help you," he said as he began to gently soap her all over.

Ruthie returned the favor, gazing down to find him fully erect. "Hmm, some-one's going somewhere," she said, her hands stroking him up and down.

He turned her around and placed her hands on the tiled shower wall. "I'll be gentle, I promise," he said as he took both her breasts in his hands, squeezing and caressing. She was already halfway to the moon when he lifted her slightly and plunged in from behind.

"Oh, babe," he said, whispering in her ear, as he took her fully and completely in a hard, passionate rutting that left both of them with shaky legs.

He helped her out of the shower and gently dried every inch of her with a thick, fluffy towel. "You okay?" he asked as he wrapped her up.

Ruthie nodded, unable to speak.

"That was amazing, babe. Are you sure you're okay?"

She nodded again. As he lifted her, kissing her softly, she said, "I've just never…I've never had sex like this before."

"Me, neither, babe."

"Why don't I believe that?"

"It's true. I saw that sweet beautiful ass of yours and I couldn't stop myself."

"I'm glad," she said, smiling shyly as she draped her arms around him and held on for a few minutes. Finally she said, "I've gotta go. Since I'm mucking stalls, it won't matter if I wear yesterday's clothes. Can you drive me?"

He nodded. "You sure you're okay? You'd tell me if you weren't okay, right?"

"Yes, but how am I gonna explain this to my parents?"

"What?"

"Not *this*, but my not coming home."

"I'm sure you'll think of something."

"Maybe, but my dad's like you. He always knows when I'm lying."

CHAPTER 17

If Nick Parker noticed the charged atmosphere in the stables that morning, he kept it to himself. By the time he arrived, Ruthie had mucked out two stalls and most of the horses were out of the barn.

Nick found her in Raffles's stall, the Friesian already out for the day. "Hey, Ruthie, fast work. Where's your truck today?"

"I walked," she lied, turning away, pitchfork flying.

"Where's the boss?"

"Maggie's not in yet and Harley's out with the horses."

"Uh-huh," he said, shaking his head, then deciding that whatever was going on was above his pay grade and none of his business.

"Hey, boss," he said, as Harley walked by, Rowdy and Royal on either side of him.

"Mornin'."

When had his boss ever sounded so chipper? "Want me to take over now?"

"Thanks, buddy. I'm actually enjoying it. I'll switch when Maggie arrives. The lesson schedule is pretty packed today."

"Okay. Are Rip and Sandy around?"

"Nope."

What had gotten into Harley? "Well, I'll help Ruthie in here, then."

"No, you won't!" she called. "Remember our agreement. I'm doin' your work till noon."

"Well, I'm not just gonna sit around."

"Enjoy, man," Harley called over his shoulder. "Grab a beer and chill."

Chill? Beer at eight in the morning? "Am I missin' something here?" he said to Ruthie.

"Harley's right. Why don't you chill?"

"Well, for one thing, I've never heard the boss use the word 'chill,' and for another, who grabs a beer at eight a.m.?"

"Mornin' everyone." They turned as Maggie walked in. "You're all up bright and early."

"Hey, Maggie," Ruthie called. "We're trying to get Nick to chill."

"Excuse me?" she said, blue eyes wide.

"My point exactly," Nick said. "I seem to be out of a job this morning."

Maggie smiled at him. "Well, if you're bored, we could really use you down the road. That is, if you don't have your heart set on chilling?"

"Thank God," he said. "Should I head down to camp now?"

"Give it fifteen minutes. Ben was getting the kids all settled with Sally. Then he's going over there directly."

"Morning, Mags," Harley said, grinning as he passed by on his way to Misty's stall.

She stared after him, a quizzical look on her face. "Did I miss something?"

Nick shrugged, winking at Maggie. "I'm gonna grab the last few horses. Then I'll head over to camp. I can always 'chill' for a few if Ben isn't there."

By ten, the stables were humming with lessons and pony camp. Maggie ran the one-week pony camp with the assistance of Rip and Sandy, the college kids they'd had working for them the past three summers. Jeb and Nick usually handled the lessons, but Ruthie filled in for Nick. She was actually a good teacher, but two of their regulars were less than enthusiastic to learn now that their handsome instructor was away.

Harley worked in the office a while, then prepared to head down to Emma's Dream. With Rip and Sandy there, the workload was lightened, at least until the pack trip group arrived. Then he wouldn't get a moment's peace. He checked in with Maggie and Jeb. "Everything okay here?"

"Fine," she said. "See you after lunch?"

"Yup," he said, but his attention was elsewhere.

She followed his gaze and saw he was watching Ruthie, his green eyes soft with affection. *Hmm, I wonder what's going on with those two?* "Harley, you okay?"

He tore his gaze away and grinned at his partner. "Great. See you in a few."

CHAPTER 18

Shortly after noon, Ruthie walked the half mile to the farm to relieve Robbie. By the time she arrived, her stomach was growling and she realized she hadn't eaten since the previous evening. After thanking Robbie and getting a status on the picking, she began rummaging through drawers and cupboards in the farm office, searching for snacks or food, but found nothing. The small fridge was empty except for a carton of half-and-half and a few cans of seltzer. *Well, I can fill up on blueberries,* she decided, not wanting to take time to run home or into town. Truth was, she was in no hurry to go home and face her mother's interrogation.

Resigning herself to a hungry afternoon ahead, she sprayed herself with sunscreen and bug spray, pulled on her wide-brimmed picking hat, and was about to head out to the fields when Leonora drove up. "Oh, Lord," Ruthie muttered. "Just what I need on an empty stomach."

Her mother emerged from her Volvo, a large picnic basket in hand. *At least I can eat while enduring the third degree.* "Hey, Mom," she said, waving as she held open the door.

"Hey nothing, young lady! You have some explaining to do! I brought lunch."

"I thought you were at the Cottage all day."

"No, Carmela and I just stayed until the furniture was unloaded. Polly and Lynn need space to organize and plan."

I know they know that, but am surprised you do, Ruthie thought, leading the way to the back porch.

"Where's your sister? I brought a sandwich for her, too."

"Out with Raoul. She ate early. I don't have a lot of time. We have a big afternoon ahead of us."

"I know, I know, slaughtering day is always tough. Sit. There's turkey and avocado, BLTs, and tuna salad."

Ruthie took the turkey, a bag of chips, and an iced tea. "Thanks, Mom. I'm starved."

"I don't wonder."

"Mom, before you start, I'm twenty-six." Recalling the night and morning, she thought, but in her twenty-six years, she had never experienced anything like last night and this morning. Just thinking about the shower made her heart race and breath quicken.

"This is different, Ruthie Ann, and you know it. Your father and I were worried sick."

"I'm sorry."

"Sorry isn't good enough! After we thought we'd lost you last winter!"

"Mom, calm down. Have a sandwich."

Absently, Leonora grabbed a tuna sandwich and unwrapped the waxed paper but didn't take a bite. "You weren't with your sister or brother. We called them. I woke poor Maggie in the middle of the night. Fortunately, Beth was up feeding Lily. We tried your friend Poppy but she hasn't seen you in weeks."

"Mom, stop! I was with Harley."

"What?"

"We were talking, it got late, and I fell asleep on his couch. I didn't come back this morning 'cause I had to be at the stables early."

"You mean at his house?"

"Yes, his condo. He lives near Polly and Lynn, by the way. It's a really nice complex, right on the river. It's where Hope and Robbie are renting."

"Well, now I've heard everything! Are you in the habit of visiting him?"

"If you must know, no. We met up in town. We were all having ice cream, Robbie got called to help Hope, and Harley offered to drive me home. We were walking to get his truck and I asked to see his place."

"Oh?"

"I was curious. I probably won't live at home forever, you know. I wanted to see what the condos were like."

Leonora took a bite of her sandwich, gazing at her daughter. Unlike her husband, she was never quite sure what Ruthie was thinking. Finally, she said, "Well, next time call, honey. Doesn't matter what age you are. We worry."

"I know. Sorry, Mom. Thanks so much for lunch. I really needed it."

"Shall I leave the basket? There are three more sandwiches. Maybe the men would like one?"

"I'm sure they've eaten, but leave the turkey and the iced teas. Chips, too. We always love to have a few snacks around."

"Don't work too hard, darlin'."

"Where's Dad today?"

"He stopped by the Cottage and then he and Spark went off for the afternoon. They've been doing this a lot lately. Disappearing to take drives and scout land. I wouldn't be at all surprised to hear that they've found a few more parcels to scoop up."

"Have to be outside the Valley," Ruthie said. "They own everything here."

"Not everything," Leonora said, hugging her. "Bye, honey."

CHAPTER 19

"Hey, partner," Maggie said as Harley walked into the barn at around five. "I figured you went straight home from camp."

"Ben and I have been talking."

"Everything all set for next week? They come in Tuesday, right?"

"I'm afraid so. I'm feeling really guilty pullin' your husband away during camp opening."

His beautiful partner smiled, removing her Stetson and wiping her brow. "We're a well-oiled machine now. I told you that last week."

Ben Morgan is a lucky man, Harley mused for the millionth time. *Woman is gorgeous inside and out.*

"Still, it's a lot."

"Not nearly as hectic as past years. The kids'll be at the Cottage with Polly and Lynn and almost all the counselors from last year are returning. It's gonna be fine. Don't give it another thought."

"Have you got a sec?"

"Of course," she said. "Let's grab a beer. It's been that kind of day."

She grabbed two Desert Ambers from the cooler, handed one to him, and sat beside him on one of two long benches. "What's up?"

"I'm going away. Tonight. That's what I was discussing with your husband."

"Where?"

"Talia's been approved for an experimental treatment. The clinic's in Palo Alto. Willow and I will drop her off. She has to be there for three nights. We thought we'd head up to Napa, to the ranch. I want to show her and talk a little about the move."

"Get her approval?" Maggie asked, smiling at him.

"Something like that."

"We'll be fine here, if that's what's worrying you. What day do you get back?"

"Wednesday. I'll drop them, then head right down. This means I'm leaving Ben in the lurch for the first day of orientation."

"He can handle it. Jeb will be here. Between him, Nick, and me, I think we can manage a few lessons. They're supposed to be a handful, but we can always ask Ruthie to help in the evenings. My dad could come over, too, if need be."

"You sure?"

"Absolutely," she said, hand on his forearm. "You have to do this for Willow, Talia, and you."

"Ben Senior stopped by camp and I told him. As you'd expect, he was fine with it."

She laughed. "So there you go. The big boss approves. Now git! It's a long drive to Flagstaff. You staying there tonight?"

"No, I'll stay a couple of hours north and pick 'em up tomorrow. Thanks, Mag," he said, tipping his hat as he turned away.

As Maggie watched him go, she wondered if he'd told Ruthie. It had been on the tip of her tongue to ask, but she had kept silent. *Not my business.* She sighed as Ben's Rover pulled into the drive.

"Hey, sweetie, you ready?" he called.

***

The Cottage was having an informal Open House to celebrate their opening. By prior arrangement, Sally Pruit brought Emma and Ben to meet their parents.

Carmela had made sandwiches and salads, and Aria Fiorelli had made an enormous cake depicting a map of the area with the Cottage at the center. Amy, Jeb, and Toby were already there when Ben and Maggie arrived. Leonora, Carmela, and Aria were bustling about in the small kitchen. As the children ran around playing and laughing, enjoying all the new toys and beautiful spaces, Spark and Ben Senior sat proudly on one of the two denim-covered sofas, surveying the chaos. Helen and Ruthie arrived together and Lang, Beth, and baby Lily a little while later.

Polly and Lynn looked exhausted but happy as they gave mini-tours. Hope and Robbie arrived just as Leonora called, "Let's eat, everyone," waving at the buffet table covered with dishes, "and drink a toast to Polly and Lynn! They have done wonders today. By Monday, when they are officially open for business, this will be the finest child care center anywhere!"

"Hear, hear!" Spark said, grabbing his grandson and spinning him in the air. Toby squealed with delight as his proud parents looked on.

"To think how he's grown since that tiny little waif who came to camp," Maggie said, leaning against her husband.

"All because of you, babe."

"And many, many others," she said, turning to kiss him.

As everyone filled their plates, Nick walked in, nodding to Maggie. "What a sweetheart he is to come," she said. "Poor guy with all these kids."

Ben laughed. "Don't let him fool you, darlin'. Parker's an old softie at heart. Hey, Shortcake," he said as Ruthie approached.

"You know I hate that name," she said, frowning at him before turning to Maggie. "Where's Harley? I thought he was coming."

Before she could answer, Ben said, "Away."

"Away where?"

Maggie observed her sister-in-law's stricken expression and thought, *something did happen last night. Oh, dear.* "It was kind of sudden, I think," she said, hoping Ben would back her up. "Talia's having some kind of treatment in Palo Alto so he and Willow are taking her, then heading up to Napa for a couple of days."

Ruthie recalled Harley's words about Talia's beauty. "All three of them?"

"No, they're dropping Talia at a clinic. The treatment takes three days. Harley thought Willow might like to see the ranch."

"What's up with you?" her brother asked. "You look like you just lost your best friend. He'll be back Wednesday."

Maggie put her arm around her. "Come on, Polly's free now. Take the grand tour with me?"

Numb and afraid she might burst into tears, Ruthie allowed herself to be led across the room to where Helen and Polly were chatting.

As Maggie and Ruthie passed by the sofa, her father took one look at her and his heart sank. *My poor baby has a rough road ahead.* When they had spoken earlier in the day, Harley told him he was still considering his offer. He asked if he could give him his answer when they returned from the pack trip and he had agreed.

"What a wonderful facility," Helen said as they followed Polly from room to room. There was the front room, dubbed the Grandparents' Lounge by Leonora, furnished with sofas and comfortable chairs. This served several purposes—as a function room and also space for parents to come and visit, nurse, or read a story. The entire room was lined with bookshelves holding hundreds of picture books. There were five play rooms. One had a water and sand table and several tables for science and craft projects. Another had sets of blocks, puzzles, large Legos, a wooden train set, and building supplies as well as shelves of toys. A third had large tables for cooking and all manner of arts and crafts as well as easels and bins of modeling clay. The fourth room was for the babies and toddlers, and had toys, bouncy seats, and soft pillows and cushions. There were also three cribs -- one for Lily, one for baby Ben, and the third for a ranch worker's two-year-old -- with plenty of room to add more, if needed. The last room was wide open with space for exercise, music, dancing, and yoga. Against the wall were cots for the older children's rest time.

The bathroom had been redone with child-height sinks and toilets, and a simple kitchen was at the rear of the building adjacent to a small office for Lynn and Polly. There were three rooms upstairs, but they had not been refurbished and were currently used for storage. Every room had walls a different color, all bright and cheerful. "We've put up some prints and pictures right now," Polly said, "but we'll soon replace them with the children's art work."

"I wish my daughter Lucy could see this," Helen said. "She runs a children's bookstore and loves to support child care centers. How many children will you have Monday?"

"Six," Polly said. "Lily is the only infant. Then we'll have Toby, Emma, Ben, and Emilio and Lorna's two girls. Christy is two and Fara is five. Emilio works up at the farm with Ruthie, Beth, and Raoul."

"Six is a good number," Helen said. "Will it be just you two?"

"Sally Pruit, Emma and Ben's sitter, has agreed to come part-time, and we'll see," she said. "Maggie suggested it and we jumped at the extra pair of hands, at least in this start-up time. We also have Heather most days. She's Toby's therapist and aide."

Ruthie listened with half an ear, a lump in her chest that felt like it was the size of a baseball. *How could he leave without saying anything after last night? Had it really been just sex? Had she fooled herself into thinking her dreams had finally come true? Stupid, stupid, stupid!*

CHAPTER 20

"This goes above and behind," Talia Goldstein said as they neared Palo Alto. Willow was asleep in the backseat of the truck cab.

"No problem. Happy to do it." Harley replied, gazing over at his impossibly thin passenger. When they had dated in college, Talia had been anorexic and bulimic, but nothing like this. Back then, he had tried to get her help, but nothing worked. Pregnancy had apparently saved her life. She'd gone home and seen a specialist, and her parents had taken care of her.

"You happy, Harl?"

He nodded.

"I only ask because you seem distracted."

"I'm in the middle of a tough decision right now."

"The new position sounds great. It's not that much farther from us, if that's troubling you."

"No."

"What, then?"

He shrugged. "It's complicated."

"A woman?"

"Yes, no… That's not the complicated part. The Valley's my home. The Morgans are the only family I have except for you and Willow."

"What about your sister, Carrie?"

"You remember her?"

She smiled. "Vividly."

"Well, nothing's changed. She and Corkie live in some kind of commune near Jackson Hole. She makes jewelry and sells 'em on the craft fair circuit."

"Don't scoff. That can be pretty lucrative."

"I won't hold my breath."

"But surely the Morgans realize what a great opportunity this is for you?"

"They do, and everyone's been incredibly supportive."

"So, what aren't you telling me?"

"My boss, Ben Morgan Senior, has offered me a chance to run a thoroughbred breeding and training farm in the Valley. He and his billionaire buddy, Spark Foster are bankrolling it and want me to be general manager. Apparently it's been their dream since college."

Talia whistled. "Talk about the chance of a lifetime, but do they have any idea how hard it is to break into that secretive, competitive business?" An accomplished equestrian, Talia had trained as jockey in her early twenties, hence the anorexia, but had dropped the idea after Willow's birth.

"Yup. They're both super competitive and totally self-made. Foster's a billionaire. His company is the largest producer of alternative energy in the world, and Ben Morgan basically owns the Valley."

"But what about studs and starting a line?"

"They claim they have contacts."

"Have they hired a vet, trainers, horse manager, anyone?"

"That's to be my job."

"Wow."

"Yeah, wow, that's what I said. I haven't mentioned it to Willow 'cause I don't know what I'm gonna do."

"Want my advice?"

"Yeah, of course."

"Take it. I can't think of anyone who's better qualified than you. Willow's been telling me about that kid, the horse whisperer. Could you take him along or any of the others? She was in love with Jeb Barnes before he got married, by the way."

Harley chuckled. "Yeah, both those guys are popular with the ladies."

"Well, I'm happy for you."

"Thanks. I feel like a shit with the folks at Hayworth bein' so great. I'm gonna talk things through. If I stay in the Valley, maybe I can come up to Napa to help out for a few months till they find someone."

"Okay, Superman. That's the turnoff, by the way," she said, pointing to a road on the left. "Now, what about your lady?"

He grinned. "Talk about complicated. Maybe on the way home."

"Promise?"

"We'll see," he said, as their daughter stirred in the backseat.

Chapter 21

Heartsick, Ruthie moved through her days at the farm like a robot. Slaughtering Day always took a lot out of them and the picking work had been especially heavy. They wanted to harvest as much produce as possible before a week predicted to have monsoon rains. Ordinarily, the verdant, fertile valley experienced regular light rains almost every night, tapering off by midmorning, but in early summer they usually had a few days or a week of torrential rains. They all prayed they would be behind them before camp opened. The pack trip had been planned after monsoon season for that reason. This year, the heavy rains were a week late.

When she thought about the night with Harley, it seemed like a dream. There were moments when she doubted if it ever happened. Beth would find her in the fields picking and staring off into space. Wednesday morning, Beth came out to see her, calling her name. Ruthie gave no indication of hearing her as she drew near, and one of the pickers shook his head as if to say, *it's not any use*, then went on cutting lettuces.

"Ruthie, hey," Beth said, touching her sister's shoulder.

"Oh, sorry, must have been daydreaming."

"I guess. I've been calling your name and you didn't blink."

"Sorry."

"We've just had a call. Ben's fallen at Emma's Dream. He's okay, but they've taken him to the hospital. Dad's gone to be with Maggie and Polly and Lynn'll keep Emma and baby Ben. Mom called and wants you to collect the kids. I'll leave Lily with Lang and go be with Maggie, Mom and Dad."

"Are you sure he's okay?" she said, jumping up, motioning to the nearest worker to collect her baskets.

"I don't know. Didn't sound life-threatening. It's his leg. They think he might have broken it."

***

Ruthie had just gotten baby Ben to bed and was reading *Charlotte's Web* to Emma when they heard the front door. Maggie stepped in, holding the door for her husband, who had a cast on his left leg from knee to toes. He was on crutches. "Hey, Peanut," he said as Emma ran to hug him.

"Daddy, Daddy, are you okay?"

Maggie looked over the child's shoulder at Ruthie, her expression grave.

"Daddy's gonna be just fine, Peanut," he said. "I'm gonna sit down and rest while you finish your story with Aunt Ruthie. Then come out and give me a kiss, okay?"

Three more chapters of a book Emma knew by heart, and the child was asleep on Ruthie's shoulder. She settled her niece on her pillow, kissed her forehead, and softly closed the door. When she returned to the living room, she found Maggie alone.

"I've put him to bed with a second dose of his painkillers."

"What happened?"

"He was up on one of the cabin roofs, repairing shingles, and he lost his balance and fell right on the leg. He fractured his tibia. They've cast it and are hoping it will heal properly, but he may need surgery if it doesn't."

"How long will it take to heal?"

"Could be six weeks, three months, or a year or more. A lot depends on an individual's healing process. They think it's a small fracture, but it's really important that he stay off it. The doctor did say that even when the fracture's healed, it will be eighteen months before the bone is at full strength. So no riding, no heavy chores, no climbing on roofs."

"Oh, Maggie, I'm so sorry."

"Me, too, but mostly I'm relieved that he's okay and it wasn't worse. They asked if he wanted a wheelchair for around the house and I was encouraging it, but you know your pig-headed brother. He flat-out refused."

"Dad and Mom must be apoplectic. Their second child to be in a cast in the last six months."

"They're fine and your mom's already in high gear, organizing meals, transportation, extra help, whatever."

"Sam and Rose come soon. They'll be happy to help." She referred to her brother, Sam Morgan and his fiancée, Rose Dillon, Lang's sister, who were flying in from Maryland for their upcoming wedding.

"My dad said he'll come to stay, too. We'll be fine. If it's one thing the Morgans know how to do, it's come together in a crisis. We'll have more help than we need and Ben can rest."

"My brother? Good luck with that."

"Your dad already said that Ben can take over more of the Lodge responsibilities. That should keep him busy. Robbie is on board to help out with the camp. Poor Robbie has been so busy working for all of us that he hasn't had a minute to figure out what *he* wants to do."

"I think he's secretly relieved," Ruthie said. "Robbie always takes forever to plan his next move. Don't ever play chess with him."

Maggie smiled. "Thank you for tonight. Emma and Ben love you so much. In all the busyness of the past month, they haven't had much time with their Aunt Ruthie."

"I loved every minute," Ruthie said.

Maggie stared at her sister-in-law, who was paler than usual and looked as if she'd lost ten pounds in the past few days. "You okay?"

"Yeah, just tired."

"Wanta talk about it?"

"He's your coworker and friend, Maggie. I don't want to put you in an awkward position."

"He's also a man, and an exasperating one at that. If it helps, I know he cares deeply for you."

"As a little sister, maybe."

Maggie smiled, taking her hand. "I think that train may have left the station a while ago. You two seem to have moved beyond the big brother, little sister stage."

"Yeah, but what stage this is this? He never called, didn't tell me he was going on this trip with Willow and her mom, and he hasn't called since he's been away."

"That's Harley."

"Whatever that means. Hey, Mag, I'd better get going. I'm sure Mom's waiting to give me my marching orders."

"Good luck with that," Maggie said.

As the front door closed behind Ruthie, she heard her husband call out. "Jesus Christ, the pack trip!"

CHAPTER 22

"There's no one else," her father said, staring across the breakfast table at her. "You have to go. Robbie isn't a strong enough rider and Nick and Jeb are needed here."

"So am I!" Ruthie said, blue eyes full of fire. "In case you hadn't noticed, it's our busiest time at the farm."

"Yes, but that's something Robbie can do," her mother said. "He's been filling in for you since he moved back."

"Filling in after getting daily direction from me is a lot different than him taking over for ten days!"

"Now Ruthie," Leonora said, "don't be so dramatic."

"I am not being dramatic. I'm sick and tired of this family treating what I do as some little hobby! I run half that farm! Who do you think is responsible for making sure that Morgan's Run produce is the best in the region?"

"We know that, darlin'," her father said. "And we couldn't be prouder, but you are the only rider on this ranch with the skills to lead this trip with this group."

"That's ridiculous!"

"They are paying a fortune. Double the usual rate. We cannot send an inexperienced rider."

"Both Nick and Jeb could do it!"

"Jeb's in school and besides, he has Toby now. Parker's an excellent trainer, but he's not the rider you are. Besides, Maggie needs them at the stables with pony camps, lessons, and the camp riding program."

"Well, I'm not going and that's that!"

She set down her fork with a clang and stormed from the room.

"Ruthie Ann, you come back here this minute!" Leonora cried.

"Leave her be, darlin'. She'll come around. I think we both know why she's balking."

"Of course we do! That Harley Langdon cannot get out of here fast enough! Has he been consulted about the change in plans?"

"I think Ben was gonna call him. Maggie's doing today's orientation with Parker's help. She's the best person to match horse to rider anyway."

"Well, don't you dare let your son go anywhere near that stable. The doctor said he needs to stay off that leg and rest!"

CHAPTER 23

Harley changed clothes and headed for Morgan's Run midafternoon. Ben had called and told him about the fall, so he was aware of the situation. His stay in Napa had been tense, but now that he'd made a decision, he felt more at ease. The owner, Kurt Hayworth, had been both supportive and puzzled. Harley had given his word to Ben Morgan that he would say nothing about the nature of his new position or the new breeding farm. Thus, he could only give the vaguest answers when asked about his plans. Finally, accepting that they had lost him, Hayworth assured him that they could manage with the staff they had until they filled his position. In the end, he had wished him luck and encouraged Harley to stay in touch.

On the way back, he had talked briefly to Talia about Ruthie, but resisted most of her attempts to learn more. Truth was, he was crazy in love with Ruthie Morgan and that scared him to death. He had always kept his relationships with the opposite sex casual. He enjoyed and liked the women he had dated over the years and there had been many, but he had never felt what he did for Ruthie. Just thinking about her unhinged parts of him he'd never known he possessed. So much of him had been shut off for so long, and now this woman he'd known all her life had ignited fires of passion and depths of feeling he'd never thought possible. *Is it too much? Will I crash and burn in any kind of relationship with Ruthie Morgan?*

"Hey, partner," Maggie said as he strolled out the back door of the barn. A half-dozen strangers were on horseback, being led around by Nick and Jeb.

"You mean to tell me we have six people who've never ridden before?" he said.

"No, only four. The other two have ridden, but they appear to be almost as green as the others," she whispered. "That's Natalie Jones," she said, pointing to a thin redhead riding Leonora's white stallion, Misty.

"Poor Misty," he said.

"She's actually not too bad. Claims to have ridden in several of her movies."

"Geez."

"The tall guy is her husband, Kai Green. He's some kind of producer."

"And some kind of old. He must be twice her age."

"And he's never ridden."

"God save us. Shouldn't someone suggest he stay home and try day trips?"

"Believe me, we tried when they made the booking. We offered all kinds of less arduous riding experiences, but they want the whole enchilada. This is supposedly a team-building trip for their next film, which has a Western setting."

"Yippee. Who are those two?" he asked, watching a pair of women struggling to stay on Tara and Raine, the stable's gentle sorrel Morgans.

She pointed to a striking woman with jet black hair and flawless olive skin. "That would be Ceci Something on Tara. She's the head costume designer. And the other one is Allison Parks. She's the head makeup artist for the new film. I predict she and Natalie'll give you the most trouble of this bunch. I haven't met the ones at the Lodge."

He studied Allison Parks -- long blond hair, sleeveless tank top, floral print capris, and brand-new boots -- and groaned. "God save us. It's gonna be a long ten days, especially without your husband. Have you figured out who's taking his place?"

"We have, but she hasn't agreed to do it."

"She? You're the only qualified 'she' I can think of and I know you're not doin' it." Maggie smiled and he said, "No! No way! I mean she's the best rider, but she can't do what we do. No way!"

"Like what? She's as good a schmoozer as your dad when she wants to be."

"I'm not talking about schmoozing, for Christ's sake. When have you ever known me to schmooze? I'm talking about picking these bozos up when they fall off their horses, setting up camp, scouting ahead."

"Ruthie's strong, she's smart, and she can find her way around these mountains better than most of us. I dare say she'd give you a run for your money."

"Who thought up this cockamamie plan, anyway?"

"Your best friend."

"Well, the fall must've rattled his brains 'cause it's a crazy idea."

"She's refusing to go anyway, so we'll see. There'll be hell to pay if the ranch has to say no to these people and refund their money."

"Jesus Christ, what a mess. Better tell me about the rest of 'em. Who are those other two?"

"Percy Fallow, the associate producer is on Annie," she said as they watched a dark-haired middle-aged man grasping the pommel in a death grip. "He was clearly terrified, which is why we gave him Annie. It took Jeb a half hour to coax him into the saddle."

Harley shook his head. "This just gets better and better."

"One bright spot—Damon Manning, the guy riding Whimsy is pretty comfortable. He's the director and pretty full of himself. Says he's ridden a few times. As you know, Martha Dillon's Whimsy's a love anyway."

"Who does he think he is, Crocodile Dundee?" Harley muttered, watching the sandy-haired man in cargo pants just out of the box and shiny new boots.

Maggie elbowed him. "Stop it! Starting tomorrow morning, they're all yours. We'll assist with the riding lessons, but you're in charge, buddy. You and whoever you can coax into going with you. Jeb can't and your dad and Ben said no to Nick. Robbie's not a strong enough rider. So if she doesn't agree, we're going to have to cancel. I just can't go with the kids and the camp opening."

"I know and I'd never ask you to."

"I'm bringing Tabasco over in the morning so I can take a few at a time around the Loop Trail."

"Good luck with that."

"Okay, fearless leader, let's get you introduced to your tribe."

"Ha, ha."

CHAPTER 24

After a tedious hour of mingling at the stables, Harley waved to the crew of beginning riders saying he'd see them soon at the welcome reception at the Lodge. Ben was planning to be there to offer a short presentation about the trip—what to pack and how to prepare. The Lodge always provided Morgan's Run tote bags chock full of trip essentials—sunscreen, bug spray, several pairs of panty hose, maps, and trail mix.

After going home to shower and change, Harley met both Bens at the Lodge at six fifteen to prepare for the group at seven. "Hey, buddy," he said, hugging his friend, who was leaning on his crutches, looking very uncomfortable. "Should you be here? Not my forte, but I'm sure your dad and I can handle this."

"I'm fine. Maggie and my mom are doin' enough mother-henning to last a lifetime, so don't you start. We need to talk."

They headed into one of the Lodge offices and chatted at length, leaving Ben Senior to greet the guests. When they returned to the lobby, he was standing with his youngest, who looked lovely in a midnight-blue sheath that flattered every curve. Her hair fell in waves around her shoulders and her silver jewelry sparkled in the evening light. Harley's chest tightened and his pulse raced.

"Hey, Shortcake, lookin' good," her brother said. "You'll have every male in the group salivating. Does this mean you've changed your mind?"

"I'm doing this for Dad, and the ranch. I would never want them to lose money on my account. Excuse me. I'm hitting the ladies' room before showtime." She brushed by Harley as she headed for the rest rooms, leaving the scent of gardenias behind.

"She's grown up, hasn't she?" Ben said, looking first at his dad, who nodded, then at his friend. "Seems a little cool with you, though, buddy. Is she still pissed you're leaving?"

Harley shrugged. "She's your sister, man."

Ben hobbled off to check with the guys setting up the screen and projector, leaving the two men together at the Lobby entrance. "Good trip west?" his boss said.

"Yup. Willow's mom did well with her treatment and I had a couple of good meetings with the management in Napa. Could we duck outside for just a minute?"

They strolled out of the Lodge to a shaded terrace, empty before the dinner hour. "I've made a decision," Harley said.

"Oh?"

"If you're still crazy enough to want me, I'd be honored to take the job."

"Excellent!" Ben Senior said, slapping him on the back. "Best news I've had all week. Wait'll I tell Spark."

"What's going on, Dad?" Ruthie said, coming up behind them.

"Just talking. Hearing about the trip west," he said, putting an arm around his youngest.

"What does that have to do with Spark?" she asked, eyeing him, afraid to look at Harley.

"Hey, I see the first of our guests now. Come on, it's now or never."

Her father hastened inside, leaving the two of them together, dangerously close. "We were talking about a new wine I found in Napa."

"Go practice in the mirror, Harley Langdon. You're a worse liar than my dad."

He grabbed hold of her arm, the touch of her smooth skin and her sweet scent enough to drive him insane. "Wait, Ruthie. Let me explain."

"Please don't. Now let go of my arm."

He released her and she stomped off, her five-inch heels clicking on the terrace floor.

He followed her in to find most of the riders he'd already met as well as the four so-called experienced riders. Among the new people was Tom Harding, Natalie Jones's co-star, brown hair, green eyes, drop-dead handsome, and didn't he know it? Guy Sorenson, the film's dark-haired, wiry stunt man, stood talking with Samantha Manning, Damon's wife. She was stunning, with long chestnut hair, brown eyes, and a slender, toned body. She was complaining that Damon would not let her bring her own horse and she hoped they wouldn't stick her with an old nag. The last person Harley met was Willa Mooney, Damon Manning's twentysomething assistant. She reached out and gave him a no-nonsense, firm handshake. Short and compact, Mooney's reddish-blond hair was cut short and freckles dotted her rosy cheeks.

When everyone had a drink, they adjourned to the meeting room for Ben's short presentation. While the women were swooning all over Harley, there were many disappointed faces when they realized that the Adonis on crutches had been replaced with his sister. However, the males in the group perked up when they were introduced to the gorgeous redhead in midnight blue.

After Ben finished talking, Ruthie said a few words about how much she was looking forward to the trip and getting to know everyone. She then announced the lesson schedule for the following day, explaining that Maggie, Jeb, Nick, and Harley would be handling the morning. Then, in the midafternoon, if riders felt ready, she and Maggie would take them on their first trail ride.

"Can't wait," Ceci said, directing her remarks to Harley.

"Can we come as well?" Guy Sorenson said. "I never pass up a chance to spend time with beautiful ladies."

Ruthie smiled. "Everyone's welcome. It's good practice for navigating on the trail."

Could she be any more of a flirt? Harley thought, watching her. *It's gonna be a long ten days.*

CHAPTER 25

Ruthie spent Friday at the farm, going over everything with Robbie and Beth. They both assured her they'd be fine in her absence. She left at two to get to the stables in time for the trail ride. When she arrived, she was surprised to see nine of the ten riders saddled up. The only one missing was Willa Mooney, who was back at the Lodge "attending to Damon's every whim," Allison Parks muttered under her breath, out of earshot of the director. "You'll see, she's his slave 'cause perfect Samantha's not gonna fill that role."

Here we go, Ruthie thought, heading into the barn to get Jadie's tack. As she walked through the darkened barn, she bumped headlong into Harley. He caught her as she lurched sideways, holding her close for several seconds before she pushed back, breathless and blushing.

"Hey, sorry. You ready to ride?"

"Yes, and I'm in a hurry."

"Jadie's all saddled. She's waiting in the west corral. Didn't you see her?" He watched the color creep up in her lovely face and he longed to kiss away her discomfort.

"No."

"Got her ready myself."

"Thanks. Well, I've gotta go."

She brushed past and Harley's chest ached with sadness and longing.

Shaken and breathless from her encounter with Harley, Ruthie took the lead with Maggie and Tabasco bringing up the rear. Jeb also rode with them, staying close to Percy Fallow, who appeared almost comatose with fear. After a day and a half, the others seemed more comfortable in the saddle.

As Nick and Harley stood watching them depart, the younger man said, "Good thing we got that second day of lessons in."

Harley shook his head.

"Two months won't help this crew," Nick said. "I predict they'll be sending a helicopter out for Fallow by day three."

"Not where we're goin'. Chopper can't get in."

"A couple are already complaining of saddle sores."

"Geez," Harley said, heading inside.

***

The next day, Ruthie met Harley and Ben at her brother's house at noon. Formerly an old homestead, the antique building had been restored and expanded by Ben and his brother Sam, an architect, creating the rambling, spectacular home it was today. Fortunately for Ben, it was mostly on one floor, planned at the time Emma was still wheelchair-bound. The house sprawled over the hillside north and south, providing some of the most beautiful views on the ranch.

"Everything's packed up," Ben was saying as the kids ran around and Maggie worked in the kitchen. "There's enough of everything for the entire ten days, but if you run low, give a call before you go through Oracle Pass and I can send the guys out."

If we make it to Oracle," Harley said. "A couple of them are still very shaky. We're gonna have to go slow."

"They all did okay on the trail ride," Ruthie said, "unfortunately, Ceci and Allison are airheads and they haven't yet grasped the importance of holding on to the reins. That's fine on the Loop Trail where Tara and Raine are comfortable, but if they pull that shit on the upper canyon trails, they could endanger the horses and themselves."

Harley cleared his throat. "We're not going that way. It's too dangerous. Ben and I reworked the route."

Ruthie opened her mouth to protest that they had not consulted her, but then closed it. They were right and she would have made the same decision if she had thought of it.

As they prepared to depart, Maggie called from the kitchen. "You two are welcome to stay. I made plenty of chili."

"Thanks," Ruthie called, "but I have to get packed and I want to turn in early."

"Me, too. Thanks, Mag," Harley called, following Ruthie out the door.

As she neared her truck, he said, "Can I talk to you for a sec?"

"I'm kind of in a hurry."

"Listen," he said, grabbing hold of her arm.

"Let go."

"Look, you can be mad or pissy all you want here on the ranch, but I'm not spending ten days out there with a co-leader who won't speak to me. It's too dangerous."

Eyes blazing, she turned to face him. "I'm a professional. Our fellow riders won't have a clue that you and I are not in perfect harmony."

"Yeah, but I will, and I need to know you have my back like I will have yours."

"Of course I'll have your back, you idiot. I love you! Now let go of me."

"Ruthie, what the hell is wrong? What have I done?"

"You never called!" she said, attempting to wriggle out of his grasp. "After that night, you never bothered to call to say you were going on your sudden trip. Never called me from the road. Nothing! Now, let go!"

She pulled away, but not before he saw the tears in her pale blue eyes. "Babe, I'm sorry, but we need to talk about this."

"We'll have plenty of time over the next ten days!" she said, stomping to her truck.

As she drove the short distance home, her tears flowed freely and she was sobbing as she pulled up at the Big House. When she looked up, she spied her father on the porch and knew he'd seen. Drying her eyes, she checked the rearview mirror and saw she was a red-hot mess.

Ben Senior rose. "Hey, darlin'. Your mom's gone into town with Helen. They should be back soon. Can you wait for dinner?" His kind blue eyes smiled at his youngest. He loved her in the special way of kindred spirits. They'd been close since she was a toddler and it had always been into her father's arms she ran when escaping from her rowdy brothers.

"That's perfect. I've gotta shower and pack anyway."

"Sweetie, you okay?"

"Same old, same old," she said, and he nodded. As she disappeared into the house, he wondered how much longer he and Spark should keep the thoroughbred operation a secret. They needed to be sure of the studs they were working so hard to acquire and they needed additional personnel before news of another thoroughbred breeding farm leaked out. Their advisors had warned them of the fierce competition they were facing if news of their plan was made public.

CHAPTER 26

The following morning, Ruthie headed downstairs at six. Her mother was already up, sitting in the living room. "Hi, sweetie," she called.

"Mama? What are you doing up?"

"Can't a mother get up to say wish her favorite youngest child a safe trip?"

"Yes, but this is way early for your maternal instincts to kick in."

"Ha, ha. It's opening day at camp. Carmela and I have been up since five. We're taking breakfast to the workers in half an hour."

"Hope it goes well."

"Sweetie, are you okay? You were so quiet at dinner. I didn't want to say anything in front of Helen, but I'm worried about you. Is this trip going to be too much?"

"I'm fine. It'll be fine. I haven't been on a long pack trip for a few years and you know I love camping."

"You know what I mean."

"It's okay. Besides, before you know it he'll be in California and out of my life."

"Yes, but is that what you want?"

"I don't have a choice, do I? Can we please drop this subject?"

"From what your dad says, this group will keep you hopping. I hope they aren't too much trouble. Try to make sure Harley doesn't lose patience. Your brother's the one who usually keeps him under control."

"I can handle him and them. Don't worry."

"Take care, my darling. I do worry about your safety, but also your heart. When you get back, let's plan a fun girls' outing. It's been too long."

"Thanks, Mama." Ruthie hugged her and headed out, grabbing a bagel and banana from one of the baskets in the kitchen.

***

Nick, Jeb and Harley were already at the stables when she arrived. All horses except for Jadie and Pepper were saddled and ready to go. The six pack mules, borrowed from a nearby farm, were loaded with provisions, tents, and water. Each rider was responsible for carrying their own clothing and sleeping gear. The bedrolls were already in place and they had given everyone strict instructions about how much they could load into their horses' saddle bags. Not surprisingly, Ceci and Allison had disregarded their instructions. Nick and Harley and were in the middle of supervising the unpacking and lightening of their saddle bags.

After a good bit of hemming and hawing, the two women began removing huge bottles, boxes, and extra clothes, some of which looked more appropriate for a cocktail party. They grumbled as they deposited the items into canvas bags provided by the stable crew.

"Don't worry, ladies," Jeb said, giving them one of his hundred-watt smiles. "We'll see that all your belongings get safely back to your rooms."

"You damn well better," Allison said, "What you've got there is probably worth a month of your salary."

"Oh, Allison, hang it up," Natalie said, rolling her eyes as she gripped Misty's mane. "I'm supposed to be the prima donna here, and as you can see, I've packed according to our guide's instructions." As she spoke, she winked at Harley. "This is not your show. You were invited along as a courtesy."

"Nat, that's enough!" her husband called.

Kai Green sat tall in the saddle. At least, *he and Royal appear to have bonded,* Ruthie thought, watching him. She was about to speak when Harley called, "Okay, okay, group."

Ruthie smiled at Parker. "You'll be glad you got rid that stuff once we get going, Ally. Remember, cowgirls travel light."

Harley watched her, grinning. *Ally indeed, but if she keeps them happy, she can get as chummy as she wants.*

CHAPTER 27

The first few days and nights were a blur. Ruthie dealt with all the women's aches, pains, and complaints, and Harley ministered to the men. They hardly spoke to each other and when everyone was settled, they flopped into their own bedrolls, exhausted, taking up positions at opposite ends of camp.

The fourth day dawned and Ruthie helped Percy Fallow to saddle his horse and pack his gear. It was obvious he would not make it for another week. "Mr. Fallow," she said softly, out of earshot of the others, "there's no shame in going back. People do it all the time."

"I never should have come. Kai bullied me into coming along. I'd have gladly stayed at your beautiful Lodge and visited the Spa every day."

"You can still do that. We'll hit cell phone range at midday and I can call and have someone pick you up. There are a few places an ATV can navigate, or if you think you can make on horseback, there's a short way back. After tomorrow, it'll be tough to turn back, so you'd have to stick it out for the whole trip."

Fallow gave her a weary smile. "Thanks. let me think about it. I'm so grateful for your kindness, Ms. Morgan."

"Ruthie, please."

"I'm sure your brother would have been a great guide, but I'm glad it's you with us."

She smiled, patting the weary man's arm. "Me, too. Now let's get you up in the saddle."

As he rolled tents and packed up, Harley had observed Ruthie's kindness to Fallow. Kai Green was in rough shape, too, but trying like heck to hide it. He found Ruthie as she was throwing the saddle on Jadie.

"Good job with Fallow," he said, aching with missing her. *If I could only take you in my arms and kiss you silly.*

She smiled. *If you only knew how much I want you right now, Harley Langdon, saddle sores and all.* "I'm guessing he'll cry uncle later this morning. What do you think? ATV or extraction on horseback?"

"I'd prefer they go on horseback, but let's see what the guys think. We'd have to keep Annie with us 'cause she'd spook with the ATV unless we ask for an extra person, and there's no way we're gonna leave them any more shorthanded back there with camp and all."

"They could really use Annie for camp," she said. "She's the gentlest horse we have. Maybe we should just tell Percy his only option is the short ride back. He's come this far. He can make it."

"Agreed," he said, touching her hand. "I miss you," he said softly.

"Me, too, even though you've made it impossible," she said, turning away to tighten Jadie's saddle, afraid she'd burst into tears.

Fallow and Kai both decided to return to the ranch. Nick Parker was dispatched to meet them. They bid the others goodbye and would wait for Nick, who was scheduled to meet up with them by late afternoon. The three would camp that night and start for the ranch at first light.

"Good riddance," Natalie said, as they headed into the pass and began climbing. She appeared to be speaking to herself more than anyone else.

Harley was in the lead, Natalie right behind him, then Samantha and Damon. The others straggled along, with Guy Sorenson and Ruthie at the rear. When not showing off, Guy flirted shamelessly with her. Most of the time thus far she had been so busy that it was easy to ignore him. Now, with Percy gone, she would be less preoccupied.

"Wanta have a bet as to which one falls off her horse first?" he said, pointing at Ceci and Allison just ahead.

"They're doing okay. Tara and Raine are pretty stable."

"More than you can say for those bimbos."

"That's a derogatory, sexist term which I hate, Mr. Sorenson."

"Guy, please."

"I would ask you not to use it again."

"Tom's boffing 'em both, you know. I wouldn't be surprised if we see some bedroll hopping on this trip."

"Mr. Sorenson, I'm really not interested in your nasty speculations and gossip."

"Sorry, babe."

"And never call me babe again!"

"Hey, honey, you work for us. I'll call you any goddamn thing I want."

"Not if you want to stay on the trip, you won't. We are here to make your trip enjoyable, but neither of us tolerates disrespect or insults."

"Woo-hoo, someone has a temper."

Ruthie reined Jadie in and slowed up to put some distance between herself and the obnoxious stunt man. From a half mile back on the wide open trail, she could still keep an eye on the two women. Willa was doing fine and rode just behind her boss.

She breathed deeply filling her lungs with the mountain air she loved so much. *I will hold my temper, but if that asshole tries anything, he'll be sorry!*

CHAPTER 28

It rained on night four and all the next day. The riders wore long ranch ponchos that covered all but their lower legs and feet. Even so, all were soggy and irritable when they made camp that night. The weather had cleared and wet clothes hung everywhere as they huddled around a roaring fire.

Once they served and cleaned up after dinner, Harley and Ruthie stepped back, ceding the fire to the others. Sorenson asked if she wanted to join him, but she ignored him and went to sit on a boulder some distance away. Harley joined her.

"Hey, everything okay? You look pissed."

"It's that asshole stunt man. He's either showing off or making sexist, insulting comments to me, or about the other women. He's a jerk."

"Want me to talk to him?"

"No, I can handle him."

"Well, we'll change up tomorrow. You know this route. You can lead and I'll insist that Sorenson maintain his position in the rear."

She gave him a weary smile. "Thanks. That would be a relief."

"I never meant to hurt you, Ruthie. I just needed time to think. I didn't want to lead you on until I figured things out."

"And did you?"

"Some."

"How is Willow's mom?"

"Okay. The treatment was tough, but they're hopeful it helped. There's no cure, but they're hoping to extend her quality of life until close to the end."

"Must be awful."

"She's strong and at peace. Tougher for her folks and Willow."

"It must have been a great comfort for them to have you there." She leaned over and rested her head on his shoulder, and he put his arm around her. His nearness and strength was so comforting, especially after enduring days of Guy Sorenson's bullshit. She closed her eyes and sighed.

Afraid to move lest she pull away, Harley sat still, his heart beating, desire rising. *All I really need in this world is this woman in my arms.* They sat for what seemed like hours until their peace was shattered by Natalie Jones's screams.

"Get it away!" she shrieked, grabbing a stick and flailing at a spot in the darkness near the fire.

With horror, Harley spied the snake just as it coiled back. "Stay still!" he cried, but it was too late. The creature struck out and Damon Manning screamed, leaping up.

Before Ruthie could move, Harley pulled out his gun and shot the rattle snake.

"Man, no one told us you'd be packing," Tom Harding said, mouth agape. Harley pushed by him and knelt beside Manning, who was shrieking, holding his arm. "I'm dying! I'm dying! Help, help!"

"Mr. Manning, you are not dying. Now, calm down," he said, as Ruthie ran for the first aid kit.

She knelt beside the two men. "Here's the anti-venom?" Ruthie said.

Harley nodded, as she handed it to him.

Guy Sorenson hovered over them, getting in the way. "Do you guys know what you're doing? I've had some first aid training and I—"

"Of course he knows what he's doing!" Natalie said, defending her tall, handsome cowboy.

Ruthie turned to face him. "Stand back, Mr. Sorenson, or I'll knock you flat."

"Come on, Guy," Samantha Manning said. "Let them do their job."

They continued to bleed the wound for thirty minutes or so. then Ruthie dressed it and put him in a sling. Later, when everyone had finally settled in and were asleep for the night, Harley and Ruthie walked fifty yards down the trail. "What do you think?" she asked. "Should we abort? He's probably gonna be too sick to ride tomorrow."

"Let's wait and see. If he needs more vials of the serum, we'll have to turn around. We only brought four with us. I'll stay awake and check on him a few times during the night."

"We should take turns. I hate for you to lose a whole night's sleep."

"Thanks. If I need you, I'll wake you," he said, hand gently brushing her hair from her face. "You're incredible, you know."

"You're pretty incredible yourself."

She spoke so softly that Harley wondered if he'd heard correctly. Taking a chance, he leaned down and kissed her, lightly at first, but as he felt her respond, the kiss went deeper and he drew her to him, drinking in her softness and warmth.

Within seconds one hand had moved down to cup her breast, the other soon dipping under her tee shirt, then her bra, to tease and caress her nipples and breasts. Ruthie groaned and he whispered, "Oh, darlin', I'd give a small fortune to make love to you right now, but we'd better stop while we can."

She nodded, cheek against his hard chest, loving the feel of him.

They walked back to camp holding hands, then separated as they came in view of the tents. "Night, my love," he whispered, wondering later if he'd actually spoken the words aloud.

Ruthie's heart fluttered. She had indeed heard his words and the tone in which he spoke. Warm and peaceful, she settled down on her bedroll.

CHAPTER 29

She had no sooner drifted off when screams pierced the night again. Once more it was Natalie Jones, but the others soon joined in. Ruthie came forward to see two coyotes standing at the edge of camp, eyeing them. They appeared to be unafraid. At the opposite end of camp, the horses reared and whinnied, hooves pawing the hard ground.

"There are eight more in the shadows," Harley whispered, coming up behind her. "They must have young nearby."

"You know what you're going to have to do," she said.

"Maybe not." He whistled softly, and within seconds Pepper was at his side. The Appaloosa was frightened, but his love for his master was stronger than his fear. Harley nuzzled him. "Here," he said, handing her his rifle. "I'm gonna try something and if it doesn't work, shoot one of the leaders. Don't hesitate, okay?"

She nodded. Ruthie Morgan was one of the best sharpshooters in the Valley. She wouldn't miss, but she sure hated to do it. These animals were healthy and strong, indicating that they had the territory they needed to hunt and breed. The coyotes weren't bothering anyone. The campers had invaded their territory.

Taking no time to fetch saddle or halter, Harley hopped up on Pepper and gave him a nudge. "Hey, ha!" he cried and charged the pack.

As the animals dispersed, Ruthie noticed Guy Sorenson, large rock in hand, at the edge of camp. Just beyond, she spied a lone coyote, separated from the pack, cowering the shadows. It was a young one. He or she seemed lost and paralyzed without the leaders' direction.

"Drop it, Guy," she cried as he raised the rock. Ignoring her, he threw it, catching the animal on the leg.

"Idiot," she heard as Harley jumped from his horse. Slowly he approached the frightened creature, who cowered and growled. "Jesus Christ, you've broken its leg." He motioned to Ruthie, who came forward, tears in her eyes, handing him the gun. As they watched, a lone shot rang out. After Harley whistled for Pepper to follow him through camp as man and horse skirted the fire.

Natalie stepped forward, attempting to pat him on the shoulder. "How awful for you."He shrugged by her, taking Pepper to where the other horses grazed. Ruthie watched, thinking she had never seen Harley so angry. When he returned, he said, "I'll stay up in case they come back."

"I'll spell you in a few hours."

"Why's everyone glaring at me?" Guy said to no one in particular. "It was a wild animal, for Christ's sake. It could have charged at any moment."

Hands on hips, Ruthie glared at him. "Coyotes do not charge! He was scared and cornered. If we'd shown him the way out, he'd have gladly joined the others. As it was, you killed him."

"Hey, I didn't pull the trigger, babe."

Ruthie watched green eyes flash with fire as Harley approached the stunt man and grabbed the collar of his shirt. "Listen, asshole, we are in charge here, not you. All of your lives depend upon us. When Ruthie tells you to drop the rock, you drop it. If there was a way to do it, I'd ship you back to the ranch now. As it is, we're stuck with you. One more stunt like that, and I'm tying you up. You can ride strapped to a mule for the rest of the trip, or maybe I'll just shoot you. Now, everyone, back to bed. One of us will stand charge all night."

Ruthie nodded to the women and Damon Manning, who still looked pale from his snake bite. "Come on. It's okay, really."

Then she asked Harley, "What're you gonna do about Manning?"

"I'll check on him in an hour or so. You sleep." His rough hand stroked her cheek. "Wish we were alone."

She turned her head and kissed his hand. "Me, too. Night."

CHAPTER 30

When Ruthie woke it was sunrise. Harley had let her sleep. She spied him stoking the fire for breakfast. Their routine was that he built the breakfast fire and Ruthie cooked. Then they switched roles at dinner. Lunch was sandwiches, trail mix, fruit, and whatever they could grab easily on the trail.

"Hey, why didn't you wake me?"

He grinned. "Truthfully? After the second check on Manning, I fell asleep. The coyotes could've eaten the whole lot of 'em and I'd have slept through it."

She laughed. "I doubt that. How is Damon?"

"Okay, no fever. He's insisting he wants to go on."

"You think that's wise?"

"Maybe not, but it's a two-day ride home from here and we'll be heading back in three anyway. Let's see how he is by this afternoon and we may be able to get phone service before we cross the river."

"Oh, God, I forgot we were going that way. No telling how this crew will handle that."

"With annoying screaming and wailing, I'm sure. Idiots, the lot of them, except the Mooney woman and Manning's wife. Only sane ones in the bunch."

"Ah, the lovely Samantha," Ruthie said. "So she's sane because she's gorgeous?"

"I said sane, not perfect."

"Harley, oh Harley!" came a call from one of the tents. "Is it safe to come out?"

"Yes, Ms. Jones," he said, giving Ruthie a look. "Perfectly safe."

She patted his arm. "Only a few more days. I better get cracking."

***

Midday found Ruthie in the lead, the Mannings right behind her, followed by Willa Mooney, Allison, and Ceci, complaining all the way. A subdued Guy followed the two women and Natalie rode behind him, taking every opportunity to ride beside Harley, "my hero." She'd spent most of breakfast talking to Damon about incorporating the "coyote scene" into their next movie and hiring Harley as a stunt double. This elicited an emphatic statement from Harley that he would have no part of such nonsense.

Damon Manning seemed to be holding up okay, though he looked a little pale. When they stopped for a lunch and water break, he insisted he was fine. Even so, Harley phoned Valley Hospital to confer about treatment and what to watch for in case Manning took a turn for the worse. As they finished eating, Ruthie stood up.

"May I have everyone's attention?" she said. "In about an hour, we'll be crossing the Gila River. After the rains, it should be high, but still passable. If you have items you want to stay dry, you should secure them now. Everyone should still have plenty of sealable bags. If you need any, just ask. River crossings can be tricky for the horses as the river bottoms are often slippery. The best way to handle them is to let them go and not try to guide them. They'll follow Jadie so you don't have to do much except stay a safe distance apart from one another. Harley will handle the spacing when we get there."

"Ten minutes, people," he said.

As they packed up, Willa Mooney approached them. "Could I talk to you for a minute in private?" she asked. Her whole body trembled.

When they had walked a short distance from the others, Ruthie said, "What's up? Are you okay?"

"I can't swim," she said, tears rimming her terrified eyes.

"Why are we just hearing about this now?" Harley said.

"I'm sorry. I didn't know we'd be going through water, much less a rushing river."

With a frown at him, Ruthie said, "It's okay, Willa. You can do this. I have a small flotation jacket for emergencies."

"You do?" he said, staring at her in amazement.

"My fiancé couldn't swim," she said, addressing her remarks to Willa. "So I had it with me on my last trip and decided it couldn't hurt to bring it along this time. What we'll do is this. You'll wear that and ride on Jadie with me. She's really sure-footed and—"

"Oh, no she won't. I'll take her. We'll be last and you can take Dandy over."

Ruthie opened her mouth to argue, but then realized he was right. Willa would be safer with him on Pepper. The Appaloosa was a good two hands taller than Jadie and much stronger.

"Okay?" he said to the frightened woman. Willa nodded and they returned to the group.

Amazed to see that every one of them was now in the saddle with no help, he grinned. "We may make cowboys and cowgirls out of you yet. Great job everyone. Just one question—is there anyone else here who cannot swim?" No one spoke up so he said, "Okay then, let's ride."

The river crossing actually went smoothly except for a few shrieks and wails from Ceci and Allison and whining from Natalie about why Willa got to ride with Harley. When everyone was safely on dry land, Willa hopped down and walked to the head of the line to collect her horse. Dandy nickered softly as she approached.

Ruthie watched woman and horse greet each other and smiled. "You guys have really bonded."

Willa gazed up at her, smiling. "Thank you."

After a late afternoon rain, they camped on high ground that night. The next morning they headed out early. At midday, they paused for lunch and to enjoy some of the most beautiful views of the trip. From their vantage point, they could see in every direction for hundreds of miles.

"That's our valley," Ruthie said, pointing to a green swath of landscape in the distance, mountains on either side.

Tom Harding stood beside her. "Pretty incredible," he said. "What's amazed me these past eight days is not seeing one other human being."

"If we continued north, we'd be in Navajo country by sundown," she said, "but we're heading south now."

"If I forget to tell you, you guys have been great. It takes a lot of patience to herd a bunch of entitled, rich nitwits across the country and keep us all safe."

"Speak for yourself, Harding," Natalie said. "I may be rich, but I'm not a snob and I'm certainly *not* a nitwit!"

Harding winked at Ruthie, then headed back to his horse.

"Okay, everyone, listen up!" Harley said as they all prepared to mount up. "As you know, we're heading south. It's a two-day ride back to the ranch, mostly flat and easy except for our descent this afternoon. This ride is by far the most dangerous stretch of our trip, but Ruthie and I talked and we decided you were ready. This is the only reason you're sitting here enjoying these incredible views. We could've skirted this ridge, but we wanted you to experience the outlook. It's the prettiest view in the Southwest."

"Especially when it's the backdrop to a shot of one gorgeous cowboy," Natalie said, snapping photos of him on her cell phone.

Ignoring her, he continued. "We'll be descending slowly all afternoon, and I do mean slowly. No one is to rush. Keep your horses reined. Is that clear? They're gonna be jittery at times and they'll need you to stay calm and steady in your seat. Comprende?" A chorus of yeses and nods greeted him. "Good. Any questions? Okay, then, let's ride."

CHAPTER 31

They began their descent right after lunch on wide trails that narrowed as they went on. To one side of them was rock wall, the other a quarter-mile drop to the canyon floor. Ruthie was in the lead with Tom Harding behind her. Somehow Sorenson had wrangled his way forward and now rode in third place, followed by Damon, then Samantha Manning. Willa followed the Mannings, then Ceci and Allison, with Natalie in her usual spot ahead of Harley.

As surefooted Jadie made her way down, the other horses followed, staying calm thanks to her lead. Ruthie steadied her at a particularly narrow spot and called back, "Remember to keep your distance from the rider ahead of you!"

The words had barely been uttered when she heard Rowdy's distinctive high-pitched neigh behind her. Peering back, she saw Tom Harding slide from the frightened horse, just barely catching the side of the cliff as he landed. Sorenson had lost focus and let go of the reins, and Raffles had spooked, nipping Rowdy's flank. Behind them, Damon and Samantha reined in Whimsy and Thor. The line behind them had stopped a safe distance back and all riders were keeping their horses calm.

Samantha jumped down and cried, "Willa, come take Thor so I can help them!"

Willa responded and Samantha inched forward, grabbing Raffles's halter. "Hey, boy, hey," she said as Sorenson sat frozen in the saddle, hands white-knuckling the pommel. Ruthie jumped from Jadie and sent her down ahead, reaching Harding as one of his hands slipped. She grabbed hold of the dangling hand, then his other arm. "Don't struggle, Tom. I'm not strong enough to pull you up. We need to stay calm till help comes. Do you understand?"

He gazed up, eyes wild with fear, and nodded. His feet could find no crevice in the rock wall and he hung limp, a hundred seventy pounds of him. All that stood between him and certain death was this brave red-haired woman, who he would surely take with him if he fell.

Ruthie felt herself slipping closer to the edge, his weight straining her arms and shoulders to the breaking point. Just as she started to go over, she felt hands grabbing her ankles. The rocking motion shook her grip, pushing her closer to the edge. Seconds from falling, she heard Harley's voice. "Get back, you idiot," he shouted as a scuffle commenced behind her.

Out of the corner of her eye she spied Sorenson shoved aside down the path. "I can't hold on any longer." She gazed down at Tom Harding and he nodded, knowing what was to come. As they began to fall, strong arms grabbed hold of Harding's arms and pulled both of them up and over the edge.

Once they were safe, Harding sat panting as Ruthie threw herself into Harley's arms, every inch of her body trembling with relief.

"Hey, hey, you're safe, sweetie. I've got you. You're okay."

As he hugged her to him, Harding sat up in time to see the wrangler kiss his partner's forehead and laughed. "Hey. Do I get one of those?"

Arms still wrapped around Ruthie, he turned to Harding. "You okay, man?"

"Now I am, thanks to you and the strongest redhead in the world."

Harley stood, bringing Ruthie with him. "Okay, let's get everyone down off this trail ASAP."

Working slowly and carefully, they took an hour to reach the valley floor. Once on flat ground, Willa Mooney burst into tears of relief, hugging Dandy. Harley and Ruthie brought out water and snacks and they rested in the shade.

Harding hopped down, then helped Ruthie as she slipped from Jadie, bone-tired, but smiling. "Thanks, Ruthie. I know you didn't have to risk your life like that. You could have let me go."

She patted his arm. "No way. We make it our business not to lose fellow riders. Besides, my partner always has my back."

"He's more than a partner, isn't he?"

She nodded. "Much more."

***

They rode for four more hours before stopping for the night. Twilights was descending as they made camp. The last night of the trip, they always tried to make the dinner special. Wine had been saved as well as freeze-dried meals prepared especially by a commercial kitchen in town. The meal included shrimp scampi, tenderloins of beef with béarnaise sauce, and several delicious vegetables that came out tasting as if they'd just been picked and lightly cooked. There was even crusty French bread, frozen fully cooked, that tasted as if it had just come right from the oven. A variety of brownies and cookies were offered for dessert. By the time coffee and tea were poured, everyone was full and happy. All except Guy Sorenson, who had grabbed a small plate, eaten, and headed out for a hike, ignoring Harley's warning to be careful.

As people headed for bed, Natalie Jones approached Harley. "Night, sugar. Now that I know you're taken, you're even more attractive." Before he could stop her, she bent down and took his chin in her hands, kissing him.

He grasped her hands and removed them from his face. "May I remind you that you're married, Ms. Jones."

"You can remind me all you want, but I don't give up easily, hon. Besides, Kai and I have an open marriage. He's probably found some maid who he's screwing this very minute back at the Lodge."

Ruthie frowned. "I doubt it. We don't have people like that working for us."

"Honey, you'd be surprised what a fistful of cash has on people's behavior. Total personality change. Kai's been known to pay tens of thousands if he wants something or someone badly enough."

Yuck, Ruthie thought, deciding not to pursue the conversation further.

Later as the others headed for bed, she and Harley cleaned up. The horses were fed, groomed, and watered and the pack mules would be loaded in the morning with trash and dirty laundry. They had planned pancakes and bacon for the final breakfast, so Ruthie secured all the ingredients in one of the food bags then hung it from a tree. When she finished her work, she went to find Harley, who was nuzzling Pepper, talking softly.

He loves that horse more than any person, she thought, watching him. "Hey, I'm off to bed, I guess."

"Oh, no, you're not," he said, leaving Pepper's side and coming to hers. "Come here, babe. You're not leaving my side tonight. Not for one second."

She smiled. "You're the only person who gets to call me 'babe,' and only when we're alone."

"I can do that," he said, drawing her close and kissing her deeply, his hands moving up and down her sides, caressing her breasts, teasing the nipples through her tee shirt until they were rock-hard and Ruthie was panting.

"Oh, oh, oh," she sighed as his lips trailed kiss down her neck. He pulled down the loose neck of her tee shirt, allowing him access to her glorious cleavage. As his tongue explored, her whole body cried out for him. Breathless, she whispered, "We can't."

"Watch me." He lifted her, moving through the pack of horses to the far side of camp, behind a stand of boulders.

They now stood in the pitch dark and Ruthie whispered, "You scouted this out, didn't you?"

"You bet your sweet ass I did," he said gruffly as he set her down and slipped off her jeans and panties. "You okay with this, sweetheart?"

While a voice screamed *Be careful, be careful,* Ruthie nodded, head on his chest. *If this is to be it, I might as well have one more spectacular night.*

His fingers parted her legs, where he found her wet and ready for him. "Oh, sweetie, are you really okay?"

"If you're not inside of me soon, I'm going to burst," she whispered, reaching down to unbutton his jeans and release him.

He leaned back against the rock and lifted her legs, wrapping them around him.

She took hold of him, gently guiding him, welcoming him, opening herself to him.

Astounded at her boldness, he said, "Whoa, baby, guess you're the boss on this one."

"Damn straight, cowboy."

His hands cradled her round, sweet ass, and he pulled her down, plunging deeper as their rhythmic dance rose to a frenzy of passion that engulfed them. They could not get enough of one another as they moved in unison to a crashing crescendo, stifling their cries of ecstasy so as to not wake the others.

As their bodies calmed, he held her, nuzzling her neck with kisses, their slick bodies melded into one. "You know," she whispered, "I'll just bet I could get you hard again."

"I'm sure you could, sweetcakes, but not tonight. You're not leaving my arms, but I think we may want to be wearing clothes. I'm sure as hell not responding to coyotes, bears, or snakes with my dick inside you."

"Hmm, I'd love to see you try."

"Not tonight, baby. Maybe another time." He kissed her again, his tongue caressing languidly now, curling round hers softly. "Much as it's gonna kill me, I'm gonna set you down." With those words and a deep groan, he lifted her and drew himself out of her warm, moist depths.

"Oh, cowboy, you are cruel," she murmured, nibbling his ear. *Was this real or just another delicious dream?*

When they were dressed, they grabbed their bedrolls and spread them side by side. Harley pulled the coarse, worn blanket he used over them and drew her close. "Good night, sweetheart," he said, kissing her on the forehead.

"Night," she whispered, feeling more peaceful and warm than she had ever felt in her life. What they had both shared might be "just sex" to him, but it was something she would remember and treasure for the rest of her life. "I love you," she said softly as she drifted off to sleep.

"I know, baby, I know."

CHAPTER 32

Knowing the pack group would be returning this morning, Maggie had left camp to come to greet them. Nick and Jeb were standing by, as were the two college kids, Rip and Sandy, and Ben Senior was on his way. "Here they come," Jeb called as he sighted the first of the riders.

Maggie stood beside him. "Oh, boy, I hate to think how exhausted some of them will be. I'll call the Lodge now to get the jeeps down immediately. Can't get them into their hot tubs and to their massage appointments fast enough."

As the first riders reached the stable yard, her father-in-law appeared with her husband. Ruthie was in the lead with two of the men behind her. The first, Tom Harding, looked none the worse for wear, but the stunt man, Sorenson, looked almost green.

"Nick," Maggie called. "I think Mr. Sorenson is going to need help."

Even though Damon Manning was in good spirits and did not seem to be suffering any after-effects or reactions from his snake bite, Raoul was standing by to transport him to Valley Hospital to be checked out. His wife appeared to be in fine shape as she hopped down from Thor, dusty but looking like she was ready to ride another ten days.

Willa dismounted stiffly and reluctantly handed Dandy over to Rip. "Bye, buddy," she said, kissing the horse on his muzzle. "Thanks for bringing me home safely."

Next came the Bobbsey Twins, as Natalie had started calling them several days into the trip. Nick caught Ceci as she slid off her horse and Allison threw herself into Jeb's arms, crying, "Thank God!"

Natalie Jones sat still as a stone, making no move to dismount until Harley drew up and hopped off Pepper. "Well, cowboy?" she said. "After throwing me over for Carrot Top, the least you can do is help me down this one last time."

Harley shook his head and went to Misty's side, raising his arms. "Let's go, Ms. Jones."

"Ms. Jones? How cruel you are! After all we've been through."

Ben Senior stood beside Maggie, watching Jones and his head wrangler. "There's gonna be some tales to tell from this one, darlin'."

Maggie laughed. "I believe you're right. Looks like our resident heartthrob has acquired another admirer."

"I'll have to talk with our PR people. We don't advertise the heartthrob aspect enough in the literature, do we? Hey, honey," he said as Ruthie came toward them. "Got a hug for your old man?"

"Sure do," she said, hugging him tightly. "It's good to be home."

Tom Harding came up to father and daughter. "Hey, Ruthie, thanks again for everything, but especially for my life."

"My pleasure," she said, hugging him.

"I'm headed straight to the hot tub, then a long nap. I'll probably drag myself to the Reception tonight. You coming?"

"Wouldn't miss it. Take care, Tom."

"I can see you've got a lot to fill us in on, honey," Ben Senior said. "Let's get you home."

"There's something I have do first, Dad," she said, heading out to the east corral, where Rip was feeding and watering Jadie. "Hey, girl, good job," she said, nuzzling the pinto's muzzle. "Take good care of her, will you, Rip?"

"No worries, Ms. Morgan."

Ruthie turned to find Harley behind her. "Hey, I'm takin' off with Dad."

"Good."

"Will you be coming to the Reception?"

"To spend more time with those pains in the ass?"

"Now, now, Willa is nice and there's always *your* beautiful Samantha."

"Let's not forget *your* Tom," he said, giving her a weary smile. "Yeah, I'll make an appearance, but a quick one. I'm bone-tired and if they don't need me here, I'm going home for a nap."

"Me, too," she said, hugging him. "I'll miss you."

She ran off before he could reply, but Harley followed her every move until she and her dad disappeared into the barn.

"So, you guys are friendly again, I see," Maggie said, placing her hand on his shoulder.

He grinned. "Somethin' like that."

"Good to have you back, partner."

"Good to be back. You have no idea how good it is to be back."

"Well, you go home. I'm headed to camp, but the guys can handle the horses and the unpacking. Go. You look like you need a nap. Then I want to hear all about it."

"Thanks, Mags," he said, tipping his hat. *All about it, except for a few X-rated moments.*

CHAPTER 33

That evening, Harley stopped by his best friend's to drive Ben to the reception at the Lodge. Even though Ben had insisted his presence wasn't necessary, he agreed to go for Harley's sake. "You owe me big time, buddy. No one wants to see an old guy hobbling in on crutches," he said as they said goodbye to Maggie and the kids. "I'm giving up family time, too."

Maggie waved her hand. "Don't listen to him. He loves it. Besides, the kids and I are going over to camp for the sing-along tonight."

"Much more fun," Harley said, ruffling baby Ben's chocolate curls. "Toast a couple of marshmallows for me, guys."

"Oh, Uncle Harley," Emma said, hugging him. "You know we can't do that. They'd be all cold and yucky."

He growled, grabbing her in a bear hug. "Just the way I like 'em!"

***

"So you had an eventful ten days, buddy. Sounds like the Manning guy checked out okay."

"Eventful's one way of putting it," Harley said. "How many years having I been doin' these trips and not one snake bite?"

"Bound to happen. What about the cliffhanger?"

"Hey, that's not something to joke about. Almost lost a man as well as your sister."

"Yeah, what exactly happened?"

"That idiot Sorenson wasn't paying attention and let Raffles get close enough to nip Rowdy. You know Rowdy. You crowd him and you get thrown. Harding went over and if your sister hadn't acted fast, we'd have lost him for sure."

"Near the top of the ridge?"

"Yup, just after Dead Man's Crawl," he said, referring to the most treacherous part of the trail.

"Maggie said Sorenson looked pretty sheepish when you rode in."

"Asshole."

"So you and Shortcake made a pretty good team, then?"

"We had our moments, but you know your sister. She knows how to ride and she knows the trails."

"So, you're getting along?"

Harley swallowed, hating to lie to his friend. They had always told each other everything until recently with the Ben Senior edict and now Ruthie. Finally, he said, "I've been meaning to talk to you about this."

"I knew it! Maggie thought there was something going on, too!"

Harley pulled up to park near the entrance to the Lodge. "Now, hold your horses. There is something going on, but neither of us have figured out what, and it would be great if we did it in private."

"Have I ever betrayed your confidence, buddy? Think about Cindy from Prescott. Did I tell anyone you guys were an item? And marvelous Marilyn, the waitress from the Bulldog? I could go on and on and you know it, buddy. Your history with the ladies has been legendary, but have I ever breathed a word?"

"This is your sister, man."

As they got out of the truck, Ben said, "Buddy, you and she have been doin' this dance for so long. We've all considered you an item for years even if you were both too stubborn and pigheaded to do anything about it. Gotta tell you, though, there's gonna be hell to pay if you take her to Napa. She's her daddy's favorite."

"There you are, you naughty boy!" Natalie Jones cried as they strolled into the lobby.

Thank you, Nat, Harley thought. Obnoxious as her greeting was, it had saved him from lying again to his best friend again. "Hey, Ms. Jones, you clean up pretty well," he said, grinning as he returned her hug.

Her face registered surprise at his unusually friendly behavior. "So do you! In fact, you two are clearly the most gorgeous men in the room, although your brothers come pretty close."

"Married," Ben said, smiling at her.

"So am I, sweetie!"

With that, she sashayed off, giving them a bird's eye view of the plunging back of her diaphanous peach-colored sheath.

"A bit on the skinny side for me," Ben whispered, "but she's got the walk down, doesn't she? You didn't tell me she was hot for you, buddy."

"Ha, ha. It's all an act, believe me. Hey, your brother and Rose are here."

"Yup, got in three days ago."

"For how long?"

"Staying the rest of the month. After the wedding, they're taking a two-day honeymoon. Then they'll be around a week or so before they fly to Scotland for a two-week hiking honeymoon."

"Bet your parents and the Dillons are thrilled."

"Don't you know it. They're staying with Martha and Jaybo until the wedding, then moving to the Big House for the last week."

The second to eldest Morgan offspring, Sam, was marrying Rose Dillon, daughter of his parents' dear friends who owned and operated Saguaro Winery on a vast property just south of Morgan's Run. In addition to the vineyard, Jaybo raised prize Angus cattle. The previous year, Rose, a pediatric neurosurgeon, had accepted a post at a clinic in Maryland. Sam had proposed, then moved with her to join a prestigious architectural firm in Baltimore.

As they scanned the growing crowd, Harley spied Ruthie on the arm of Tom Harding as the pair stepped in from the terrace. Drinks in hand, they were chatting amiably. He frowned. *Who the hell does he think he is?*

"Hey, buddy, looks like you've got some competition," Ben said, grinning from ear to ear. Whatever was going on between his sister and the man standing beside him, Ben was only too aware that his friend sometimes needed a nudge or two in affairs of the heart. "You know what they say about near-death experiences. They can forge incredible bonds between the survivors."

Harley frowned. "My guess is Mr. Harding bonds with a new woman every week."

"Hi, Harley," Willa Mooney said, passing by on her way to the bar.

"Hey, Ms. Mooney. You remember Ben Morgan?"

"Yes, hello."

"So, how was the trip?" Ben asked, smiling at her.

"Actually, it was wonderful. I never thought I could do something like that, but I did it. I loved riding and I love sweet Dandy. I'd love to meet Mr. Dillon, the owner, and tell him how great she was. Is he here?"

"Unfortunately, Jaybo's health isn't the greatest. That's one of the reasons Whimsy and Dandy spend ninety percent of their time in the Morgan's Run stables instead of at the vineyard. No one ever rides them over there. Jaybo seldom ventures far from home, but if you want, one of us could take you down to the vineyard before you go?"

"Thanks. I'd love that if I wouldn't be intruding and if Damon doesn't need me."

As she walked off, Harley said, "She's Damon Manning's slave, poor woman. Never gets a moment to herself. I think she was more upset about his snake bite than his own wife."

"Speak of the devil," Ben said, spying Samantha Manning from across the room. In a black dress that hugged her slender frame, the director's wife hair had pulled back her thick, dark hair with silver combs. "She certainly a looker."

"And she knows it. Can't complain too much, though. She was great on the trip. Even without her fancy riding habit, the lady can ride."

The senior Morgans arrived and Leonora immediately began fussing over her eldest. "Maggie says you should be sitting, darlin'. Let's find a place where you and your dad can park yourselves."

"Now, Nora, we're not ready to be put out to pasture yet."

"Is Spark coming tonight?" his son asked.

"Nope. First night of the Barnes visit so they're havin' a family dinner."

Harley's attention wandered as he followed the movements of Harding and Ruthie. They were still arm-in-arm, now chatting with Kai Green. She wore silver jewelry and an off-white sheath that fit her curvaceous body like a glove. Harding continually found reasons to run a proprietary hand up and down her back or along her side. The dress's short skirt and her five-inch heels showed off her glorious legs, which Harley wished were wrapped around him, his cock where it belonged, deep inside her.

"Would you excuse me?" he said, heading in her direction.

"What's gotten into that boy?" Leonora asked. "He's usually hugging the wall at these things."

"The green-eyed monster," Ben said.

His father laughed as Leonora said, "It's about time someone lit a fire under that man's you-know-what! Tom Harding is nice-looking. A step up from some of her recent beaus!"

CHAPTER 34

"Ruthie, have dinner with me tomorrow, please," Tom said. "It's only dinner and I'd like to repay you somehow."

"There's no need."

"Well, I think there is, and you'll save me from another boring meal with this crew. I mean, I love 'em, but after ten days together, I'm ready for a break."

"May I remind you that you also spent the last ten days with me."

"Ah, but it was our *first* ten days, like a honeymoon, so to speak. Come on, what'd you say? It's just dinner, not a marriage proposal."

"Okay, I'd love to."

"Great. How bout I pick you up at seven?"

"Perfect."

"Uh, oh, someone is headed our way and he does not look happy."

Ruthie turned to see Harley halfway across the lobby, a frown creasing his handsome face. In a dress shirt and nice jeans, he looked even more gorgeous than usual, and she felt her breath quicken. "Hey," she said as he neared them.

"Hey, yourself. Harding." He nodded. "How're you feeling?"

"Not bad. A whirlpool, sauna, massage, and nap and I'm a new man except for my arms. They feel like they've been stretched a foot longer."

"That'll pass," Harley said.

"The Spa actually has a treatment that targets the arms," Ruthie said. "You should check it out."

They were soon joined by Natalie, Kai, and the others, and Ruthie stepped away. "Will you excuse me? I haven't seen my brother Sam in nearly six months."

Despite her husband's presence at her side, Natalie grasped Harley's left arm. Even had he wanted to follow Ruthie, he would have had to cause a scene extracting himself from her death grip. He gave in to the inevitable and watched as she threw her arms into her brother's arms.

"Sam!"

"Hey, sis, lookin' good."

She blushed. "Thanks. Hi, Rose, so good to see you!" She hugged her soon-to-be sister-in-law, of whom she was very fond.

"We're glad to be home," Rose said. "Sam's right. You're looking very well, especially after ten days on the trail."

"So, how are you two? Tell me all about Baltimore," she said, all the while observing Harley out of the corner of her eye. *Could Natalie Jones be any more obnoxious?*

***

As the most of the party headed in to dinner, the Morgans began to disperse. Everyone was invited to the Big House for sandwiches, but Sam and Rose begged off as they'd promised to dine with her parents and her brother Lang, Beth, and Lily. Robbie and Hope were headed to the Bulldog. Helen and the elder Morgans found Ruthie saying goodnight to Tom and asked if she wanted a ride. She declined, telling them she wanted to walk home. She loved the path that led from the Lodge to the Big House. At this time of year, it was particularly beautiful at twilight when the lightning bugs came out. *The stars fallen from the sky*, her mother used to tell them.

After saying her goodbyes, she walked out the rear entrance and was just removing her heels when Harley caught up with her. "Got a minute?"

"Oh, you startled me! I'm surprised you could extract yourself from *your* Natalie."

"Don't start. And, you should talk. You were falling all over Harding."

"Don't be ridiculous. He's just grateful, that's all."

"Yeah, right, and I'm the Easter Bunny."

"Well, I like him," she said, chin jutted out, the old stubborn Ruthie rearing her head. "He's a friend."

"Need a ride home?"

"No thanks. I'm walking."

"Wanta grab dinner with me?"

"Where?"

"I don't care. In town? Wherever you like."

She hesitated, then said, "Okay."

He gave her a look. *Okay, two can play at this game.* "My truck's over here."

As they drove into town, he said, "Gracie's okay? Or we can go to the Bulldog?"

"Let's get Gracie's takeout and eat in the park."

"Okay, you gonna want wine or beer? I can stop."

"I've had enough, thanks. I'm actually not that hungry. Maybe I'll ask her to make a half sandwich for me."

"Okay."

They took their food to the park in the village green and sat on benches near the wooded area at its far end. It was a lovely night, a slight breeze blowing. Cries of laughter reached them from the opposite end of the park. Near the large playground, several families sat at picnic tables, the children running back and forth from table to jungle gyms and swings.

"You look beautiful, by the way," he said, his fingers tickling the side of her hand.

"You look pretty great yourself. It's not often we get to see Harley Langdon dressed up. Weddings, funerals, that's about it."

"I could say the same thing about you."

She shrugged. "Tom Harding asked me to have dinner with him tomorrow night."

"Of course he did. What did you say?"

"Yes."

"Why?"

"Because he's a guest and a friend and it would have been rude to say no."

"You know what he wants, don't you?"

"Yes, to have dinner."

"And afterward to divest you of whatever sexy outfit you're wearing."

"Well that's not happening."

"How do you know?"

"If I have to answer that after our recent past, I'm going to squish this sandwich in your face, Harley Langdon. What do you take me for?"

"A woman who doesn't realize the sexy bombshell she's grown into."

"Sexy bombshell? Is that how you think of me?"

"No…yes…sort of. You know what I mean."

"Are you just using me for sex?" she said, turning to gaze into his green eyes.

"Is that what you think?"

"Sometimes. I mean, the sex is amazing, but there doesn't seem to be more. I know you don't do anything hastily except to accept a job a million miles away without telling anyone, but still."

"Truth is, I've never had more than a casual relationship with a woman and now my kid sister is also my lover. It's a lot to digest."

She stared straight ahead and said nothing.

"You're mad, aren't you?"

She shook her head. "I made up my mind that if you were leaving I'd take you any way I could get you. Do you know how many years I've dreamed about sex with you? And never in my wildest dreams did I think it could be as great as it's been. I guess if it's gonna be a dead end, I'm still glad we did it."

"Ruthie," he said, taking her hand.

"I think I'm ready to go home now, okay?"

"You sure?"

"Yup."

They drove home in silence. As he parked in front of the Big House, he reached over and attempted to take her in his arms, but she slipped away. Once outside, she poked her head through the window. "Night. See ya."

Before he could reply, she ran into the house and shut the door.

CHAPTER 35

The elder Morgans and Helen Winthrop were in the living room as Ruthie banged in the front door and ran upstairs.

Leonora sighed. "Oh, dear, trouble in paradise and I'll just bet his initials are H.L. That man cannot leave the Valley fast enough, in my opinion."

"Now, Nora, it's not entirely the boy's fault. Our baby can be volatile. I love her, but she does have a temper."

"He seems like a very nice man who's working hard to figure things out," Helen said. Both Morgans stared at her and she smiled. "I'm not certain how we got on the subject, but Harley and I had a nice talk the other night about transitions, his and mine. He was actually very kind and understanding."

"Harley's a good man," Ben said. "As I'm sure Nora's told you, Ruthie's been pining away for him most of her young life. If you'll excuse me a minute, I'll go up and offer my shoulder."

"Yes, go, darlin'," Leonora said. "You're the only one she listens to."

He knocked on the door and received no answer, but could hear sobs within. "Hey, baby, got a minute for your old dad?"

No answer.

He pushed open the door and found her collapsed in a heap on the bed.

"Hey, sweetie, can your dad give you a hug?"

Ruthie sat up and threw herself into his arms. "Oh, Daddy, I've made such a mess of things!"

"I doubt that, honey."

"Well, I have."

"My guess is, this is exhaustion talkin'. You've been on the trail for ten days, you nearly fell off a cliff, and you feel like your fella's deserting you."

Of all their children, Ruthie had the personality that did an about-face when she was overtired. When she was a child and tired, the temper tantrums came, fast and furious ones that lasted for hours. At such times, it was her father who calmed her down and put her to bed.

She sniffed, leaning her head on his warm chest. "I love him and he…he…he never says anything. I know I should just put him out of my mind, but I can't and now he's leaving! Even if we've never been together, Harley is as much a part of me as you, Mom, my brothers, and Beth. I don't know what I'll do when he's gone."

"Dry your tears, sweetie. I'm gonna tell you something now, but only if you swear that you can keep a secret."

She pulled back and stared up at him, curiosity in her red-rimmed eyes. "What are you talking about?"

"You have to swear to keep a secret, honey. It's really important not only to me, but to Spark."

Ruthie stared at her father as if he had sprouted horns. "Of course, I swear."

"That means you can't say anything, even to Harley."

"I swear."

"Your fella's not goin' anywhere. He's stayin' to work for me, for Spark and me, in a different capacity. We're are starting up a thoroughbred breeding and training farm. Work's been goin' on up on the northern part of the ranch for six months."

"Does Mom know?"

"No one knows except Harley. Spark and I had to tell him because we needed him not to head off to California on us. We've hired him as our general manager."

"I can't believe it. Mom's gonna kill you when she finds out."

He chuckled. "I hope she'll be pleased before she takes the ax to me."

"So how long before you tell her?"'

"We were gonna wait a few months, but now that Harley's accepted the position, we're plannin' to tell everyone after the wedding. We don't want to steal Sam and Rose's thunder."

"Can I see it?"

"Will it cheer you up?"

"Absolutely."

"Then we'll take a drive down there this week. Maybe in the early morning or evening before or after work?"

"I'd love it."

"Now, remember—not a word to anyone. Promise?"

"I do," she said, hugging him, so pleased he had confided in her.

"Get a good night's sleep, honey. I know they're eager to have you back at the farm. Robbie's been workin' hard, but it's not the same as having you there."

"Thanks for saying that, Daddy."

As she drifted off to sleep, she realized she hadn't asked her father when Harley had accepted. No matter when it was, it didn't matter. Knowing that he was staying gave her the first peaceful night's sleep since she'd heard about Napa.

CHAPTER 36

Ruthie headed to work at seven, taking the huge basket of lunch Carmela had packed for her and Beth. Glad to be back, she plunged into the work. The gardens looked healthy, but in need of her care. Robbie had held down the fort, but he was not a farmer. By noon, she had begun to feel slightly caught up. She met up with Beth and they settled on the porch, opening Carmela's feast and pulling out baguettes filled with chicken salad and all kinds of greens.

"Bless you, Carmela," Beth said, sighing as she took a bite. "We had nothing in the fridge today except peanut butter and moldy cheese. I needed this."

"Me, too. It's amazing what a good night's sleep and great food will do for a person," Ruthie said.

Beth eyed her. "So, how's everything? How'd you and you-know-who do on the trip?"

"It was fine. We were so busy with that crew that we barely saw each other."

"And when you did?"

"It was fine, and sometimes more than fine." She smiled at Beth, wanting so badly to confide in her, yet holding back, not yet willing to reveal how far she'd gone or how deep into the relationship she'd stepped.

"When you're ready, I want details," Beth said. "In the meantime, if you're all over the place and he's turned you inside out, don't forget there's always my therapist, Haley. You remember how much she helped me after Lily was born, and earlier? She's truly a lifesaver."

"Thanks, sis," Ruthie said. *Truth is, now that I know he's staying, I can endure anything.*

"You seeing each other tonight?"

"Nope. I have a date tonight, with Tom Harding, one of the Hollywood crew."

"I know him. We watched one of his movies the other night. He's hot."

"And doesn't he know it. He's a great guy, but we're just friends."

"Even so, your date'll give Mr. Can't Commit something to think about, won't it?"

Ruthie grinned. "Maybe. Either way, I'm gonna have fun tonight and put Harley Langdon out of my mind."

"That's the spirit!" Beth tossed her sandwich wrapper into the trash. "I've gotta get going. I'm meeting a potential new buyer in ten minutes and he wants to see the livestock."

"We cleaned the chicken coops this morning, so bring him on!" Ruthie said, waving goodbye, her spirits lighter than they'd been in weeks.

CHAPTER 37

After work, Harley headed home to shower and change. Ben and Maggie had invited him to dinner. He suspected that his friends knew he would be going crazy imagining Ruthie with the handsome movie star, and they were right. *It's only dinner,* he told himself, but he'd seen the way Harding looked at her. *This isn't one of her Internet dates who she parades by me and the family. Tom Harding is a real threat.* He had no idea where they were eating, thank God, or he'd have been tempted to storm in and carry her off. By the time he arrived at Maggie and Ben's, he had worked himself into such a state that he wondered if he'd be able to have a normal conversation.

Emma and baby Ben greeted him at the door with shrieks of delight. "Uncle Harley! Wanta play tag?" Emma cried, hugging his waist as little Ben wrapped chubby arms around one leg.

"Sure do, but maybe we should go in the back yard. What'dya think?"

As the three of them raced through the kitchen, Harley waved at their parents.

"Don't worry, buddy. I'll spell you in five minutes and I'll bring beer," Ben said.

After dinner, Maggie put baby Ben to bed and allowed Emma to watch a short movie she loved. She joined the men, who sat in the front porch rockers. She settled on the swing, leaned back, and sighed. "Between the stables, camp, and those two, I am pooped. Fortunately being at the Cottage wears out our little devil. He's asleep when his head hits the pillow."

"Beer, baby?" her husband said.

"No, thanks." She closed her eyes. When the silence continued, she sat up, wondering if she had interrupted a conversation between the two friends. "If you guys want to talk privately, I can go inside."

"Absolutely not, partner. There's nothing about this sad tale that you can't hear. I'm just a dumb son-of-a-bitch, that's all."

"No, you aren't," she said. "You just don't have much practice with this kind of thing."

"I don't know about that, hon," Ben said. "This guy's dating history is legendary."

She reached over and patted her husband's arm. "Dating, maybe. Loving, settling down, committing? Those are very different things, sweetheart."

"As always, Maggie's right," Harley said. "I've perfected the art of love 'em and leave 'em relationships, but this thing with your sister is a different animal. Excuse the awful mixed metaphor"

She smiled at him. "You'll figure it out. It took Ben and me a while, if you recall?"

"I may not get the chance if Tom Harding swoops in and steals her away. What an idiot I've been."

"Will you listen to this lovesick cowboy, sweetie? He's completely lost his senses," Ben said.

Maggie smiled. "I'll say! Harley Langdon, Ruthie has loved you since she was in diapers. Do you think some Hollywood heartthrob is going to steal her heart in one night?"

"Maybe not, but I can see her sayin' 'enough with a certain stupid cowboy' and starting over. Don't s'pose you two know where they're eating?"

Maggie chuckled. "No, and if we did, we wouldn't tell you for fear you'd charge in there like a madman."

"Saving me from myself, huh?"

Ben laughed. "Got you covered, buddy. Always."

*****

As they sipped an excellent sauvignon blanc, enjoying the views on the Red Mesa terrace, Tom Harding reached across the table and took her hand. "Do you ever take vacations?"

"Sometimes," she said withdrawing her hand. *This evening may have been a mistake*, she thought as they sat in the most romantic restaurant in the Valley.

"I'd love for you to come to LA with me. We could charter a boat and cruise the coast or fly to Hawaii for a few days or drive up to Carmel or Monterey."

"While all that sounds amazing, Tom, it's also something you do with a significant other."

"Which you are to me. The woman who saved my life deserves to be treated like a queen."

His dark green eyes sparkled as they gazed at her. Dressed in beige linen suit, dapper bow tie, and pale blue shirt, he looked every bit the movie star he was. A real catch. A month ago, she'd have jumped at the prospect of a relationship with him, but now, after the past two weeks, it was impossible.

"This wine is delicious."

"Only the best for the woman who saved my life. We're bonded forever, you know."

"Technically, Harley Langdon saved both our lives."

"Not mine. If you hadn't caught me first he would never have reached me in time."

"Okay, a joint effort. Do you feel bonded to him, as well?"

"Nope, just you."

His eyes told her everything she needed to know. "Tom, this is really nice of you. Red Mesa is the best restaurant around and I do enjoy your company, but only as a friend."

"Got your cowboy on your mind, huh?"

"Something like that."

"He's an idiot if he hasn't asked you to marry him."

"He's a slow mover."

"Honey, I doubt that very much. Langdon's a player. A lady's man if I've ever seen one."

"Maybe."

"No maybes about it. I'm assuming you only consented to dinner tonight to make him jealous."

"No, that's not true! I consented because you're a friend and you asked me."

"Well, I asked you because I like you and wanted more."

"I'm sorry." *You don't know how sorry I am!*

"Well, we can certainly enjoy this beautiful spot. I hear the food is excellent."

"It is. Thanks."

"For?"

"For understanding."

"The night's not over yet, sweetheart."

CHAPTER 38

Ruthie was knee-deep in romaine lettuces when she spied Harley's truck speeding up the farm drive. *What the heck does he want? Probably to heckle me about last night!* The evening with Tom ended amiably. When he left her at the Big House, he walked her to the door and kissed her on the cheek, a chaste, friendly kiss. *So Mr. Jealous has nothing to hassle me about!*

She decided to stay put rather than running up to meet him. She turned back to her work and waited. She did not have to wait for long. She heard his footsteps, but kept picking, tossing perfect heads of lettuce into her basket. As she stood to signal the pickup cart to collect her baskets lined up in a row, he reached her. "Hey."

"Hey yourself. What are you doing here in the middle of the day?"

"I wanted to talk to you."

"Can it wait? I'm really busy today."

He wanted to shout, *No, it can't wait,* but instead said, "Fine, how about after work? Drink or dinner? Bulldog?"

"Okay, which?"

He looked at her quizzically. "Which what?"

"Drink or dinner?"

"Whatever works for you."

"Okay, let's have a drink at the Bulldog and see if we feel like dinner."

"When should I pick you up?"

"I'll meet you there. Seven okay?"

"Seven's fine." He shuffled around a bit, feeling awkward and a bit foolish.

"Well, I'll let you get back to work."

"Okay, see you later," she said, stooping to continue her picking.

Harley Langdon taking time out of his day to come to the farm and ask her out? Stranger things had happened, but she could not think of one.

CHAPTER 39

Ruthie walked into the Bulldog, the only saloon in town, a little after seven and spied Harley at the bar talking to Russ Keeler, the owner. The dark, wood-paneled bar was a popular watering hole for tourists and locals, its walls lined with black-and-white rodeo photos, many featuring local wranglers including several photos of Harley Langdon as well as a number of Ned Williams, Maggie's dad.

"Hey, Carrots," Russ called as she approached. Ruthie was a favorite of the saloon owner. Before taking over at the farm, she had been his best waitress.

"Hey, Russ."

"What'll you have?"

"DA'd be great, thanks." She referred to a local microbrew, Desert Amber, commonly called DA.

"You guys eating dinner?"

Harley looked at her .

She looked up at the board. "I'm starved, so I vote yes."

"Guess we are, Russ."

"You know what you want?"

"Bulldog Burger, medium rare," she said.

"Make that two," Harley said, "and I'll have a green salad as my side." "Curly fries for me," she said, sliding onto a bar stool.

"I thought we'd take a booth," he said, indicating one in the back.

She shrugged. "Fine with me." She hopped up, beer in hand, and sashayed toward the booth.

"What's she high on tonight?" Russ said.

"Life," Harley replied drolly as he turned to follow.

Sliding in opposite her, he said, "How are you?"

"Tired. It was a long day."

"Have fun last night?"

"Yes, as a matter of fact. You said you wanted to talk?"

Green eyes flashed fire. "What happened with Harding?"

"I could say it is none of your business."

"Don't be ridiculous and don't get cute with me, Ruthie Morgan."

She smiled coyly. "You jealous?"

He grabbed hold of her hand. "What do you think? Are you gonna tell me or do I have to beat it out of Harding?"

"Now who's being ridiculous?"

"Are you seeing him again?"

"Well, yes, and so are you. Have you forgotten the farewell dinner tomorrow night?"

"Oh, Christ," he said, shaking his head.

Ruthie watched him for a minute, then said, "Nothing happened. We went the Red Mesa. The food was terrific, we had a nice dinner, he brought me home, we said goodbye, and that was it."

"I don't believe you."

"Well, that's your problem, not mine!"

At that moment, Russ brought their food. Ruthie looked up at him. "Thanks, Russ. I'm not feeling very well so I think I'll take this to go. Can you please box it up?"

"Sure thing. You too, Langdon?"

Harley nodded. "Why not?"

He walked her to her truck, which was in the Bulldog lot. At the door, she turned, gazing up at him. He still looked angry, but there was also sadness in his beautiful green eyes. "Are you really as dense as you sounded back there?" she said softly. "Do you want to know why nothing happened? *You*, that's why. Harding knows how I feel about you even if you don't. I couldn't sleep with him, or even kiss him, after what's gone on between you and me since that night at your condo. Maybe someday you'll figure it out."

"Ruthie, wait."

"Night, Harley," she said, hopping in and shutting the door. *This I know how to do—be angry at that stubborn stick-in-the-mud! As long as he's staying in my life, I can do this till the cows come home. See how he likes it!*

CHAPTER 40

"Hey, partner," Maggie said as she spied Harley in the stable yard, the early morning sun already oppressive. "It's gonna be a scorcher. You okay here? I'm only stopping by. Jeb and Nick are doing today's lessons. I've got a million errands to run for the rehearsal dinner. Leonora's given me a list a mile long."

"Hey," he said, tipping his hat.

They always took a week break between the two camp sessions and Rose and Sam had planned their wedding during the hiatus so as not to drive everyone crazy.

"If you've got any chores for me, I'll be back by one."

"No prob. Say, Mag, got a sec?"

"Of course." She paused, gazing over at him. He looked terrible. "Everything okay?"

"No. I haven't slept in two days and I feel like shit. I'd ordinarily be talkin' to your husband about this, but he's been so socked in with your dad up at the Lodge that I haven't been able to grab him."

"What's going on?" she asked, sitting down on one of the wooden benches in the shade.

He sat beside her. "You really like that Alvarez woman, right?"

"You mean Haley, my therapist? Therapist to the Morgan family, really?"

He nodded. "Think she'd see me, I mean a man?"

Maggie smiled. "Yes, she sees both men and women. And to answer your question, I love Haley. She has saved my life on several occasions."

"I've gotta do something, Mag. I'm literally going insane here."

"Got your cell on you?"

She told him the number, which he added to his contacts. "Thanks, partner."

"No problem. Call her today. She might have time."

As soon as Maggie departed, he dialed Haley's number, afraid if he waited, he'd chicken out. He got her voice mail and left a message. Within an hour, she called and agreed to see him that evening. He rung off and went back to work.

***

"Where are you two off to?" Leonora said as Ruthie and her father headed out.

"Just doin' a few errands in town," he said.

"Wait a minute! If you're going into town, I have a bunch of things you can do for me."

"Whoa, Mama," she said, "This is a quick trip. I have to work, you know."

"Not after tomorrow. Ruthie Ann, remember, you promised Thursday through Sunday you are mine."

"You'll have me, Mama, but we've got to get going."

"Maybe I'll come along."

"Aw, darlin', you'd be bored silly at the feed and grain and hardware store."

"That's where you're going? Why is Ruthie needed at the feed and grain?"

"Now, darlin', can't a father spend a little time with his baby without the third degree."

Leonora waved. "Oh, pish tush. Go! I know when I'm not wanted. You two have always been thick as thieves."

Ben Senior gave her a kiss. "Not as thick as we are, darlin'."

Ruthie watched them. Like all her siblings, she wondered if she would ever find love like theirs. It was an impossibly high standard.

"You're getting to be an accomplished liar," Ruthie said as they drove north out of town.

"I know. I feel terrible lying to your mom, but all will be revealed soon. I hope she'll be pleased."

CHAPTER 41

Rose's wedding gown and bridesmaids' dresses had been made by Gabriela and her crew. Rose had chosen a pale pink silky fabric with a faint floral swirly print for the bridesmaids, but Maggie, Beth, Ruthie, Amy Foster-Barnes, and her maid of honor, Sadie Thomas had been free to choose the style they liked best. Leonora and Martha Dillon had gone to their favorite dress shop in Prescott for their coordinating dresses. The groomsmen and fathers were wearing dark blue suits with ties, also from Gabriela's, made of the same cloth as the bridesmaids' dresses.

After work, Ruthie cleaned up and swung by to pick up Beth for the trip to town to collect their dresses.

"Hi ladies," Gabriela said as they stepped into the cool, dark recesses of the dress shop. "The bride left fifteen minutes ago with her dress. Simply gorgeous! Now let see to you two."

Beth had picked a simple A-line sleeveless sheath. She slipped it on and it was perfect. "That gorgeous husband of yours is gonna love it, sweetie."

"You don't think it's too tight in the bust?" Beth asked, turning from side to side in front of the mirror.

"Absolutely not! Like so many nursing mothers, you look glorious."

Ruthie was behind her sister, shaking her head at Gabriela, but the dressmaker didn't notice. Her sister had struggled to nurse Lily until finally, frustrated and disappointed, she had given up and switched to bottle feeding.

Beth's face fell. "Well, that wouldn't be me. I was a failure at nursing. I just must be fatter."

"Aw, hon, I'm sorry. Dumb comment. You always did have a perfect bust line for this type of dress. Does it feel okay? I can let it out, but I think you look perfect."

"No, it's fine. You're right. Lang will love it, even though we're meant to be pleasing the bride. Your turn, sis."

Ruthie popped into the dressing room and emerged in an off-the-shoulder dress, cinched at the waist, with a flared skirt and a neckline that revealed more than a hint of cleavage.

"Wow, that dress was made for you, sis!" Beth said as she and Gabriela stared openmouthed. Ruthie was all curves with a tiny waist and a lovely bust line.

The dressmaker clapped her hands. "And I'm the one who made it. What'dya think, hon?"

"I love it, although my mother won't. Guaranteed. You don't think it's too tight? Do I look slutty?"

"Absolutely not!" Gabriela cried. "I do not create slutty dresses!"

"Beth? Be honest. Will Mom freak?"

Her sister grinned. "No…maybe, but who cares? I know who will freak for sure. A certain wrangler's gonna be drooling the second he catches sight of you."

Ruthie beamed. "Has Maggie picked up her dress?"

"Yes, and hers is similar to yours," Gabriela said. "She looks gorgeous, but then, you gals would look gorgeous walking down the aisle in potato sacks."

"Yup, the two bombshells and skinny ole me," Beth said with a smile on her face.

"Nonsense! *All* of you are beyond beautiful!" Gabriela said. "The maid of honor is coming in tomorrow, I understand. I'm hoping the measurements she sent were accurate. Let me bag up these dresses. The shoes are there, too."

After depositing their dresses in Ruthie's truck cab, they headed to Gracie's for dinner. When they emerged, stuffed full of her evening special of trout and a savory flan of summer vegetables, they decided to get cones at the Daily Scoop.

As they turned the corner toward the ice cream shop, they almost ran into Harley, who appeared to be looking for an address.

"Hey, Harley, you look lost," Beth said, smiling.

To their surprise, the handsome cowboy blushed crimson. "Nope, just noticing the architecture." He tipped his hat. "Have a great night, ladies." He hurried around the corner out of sight, leaving the two women staring after him.

Beth looked at her. "What was that all about? I've never seen him act like that."

"Me either," Ruthie said, shaking her head, wondering if they should follow him and see what he was up to.

"Come on," her sister said. "My two scoops of Rocky Road are waiting."

***

Embarrassed after his run-in with the Morgan sisters, Harley was completely discombobulated when he stepped into Haley Alvarez's waiting room. The woman herself was sitting in an easy chair as he closed the door behind him. "Hi, Harley, good to see you again," she said, rising and extending her hand.

"Hello," he said, returning her firm grip. "Thanks for fitting me in on such short notice."

"Come on back. Can I get you something to drink? Water? Juice? Soda? Tea?"

I'd kill for a beer. "Thanks, I'm fine."

"So how can I help?" she asked after they'd settled.

He had met Haley at Beth Morgan's wedding. Today, with her waist-length hair loose and flowing over a wide silver caftan, she looked like Mother Earth.

"I don't know where to start."

She smiled. "How about today?"

Before he knew it, Harley had launched into his sleeplessness, his relationship issues with Ruthie, his rootless nature, and his inability to commit. By the time the hour was up, he was talking about his father. Haley gazed at him, her gray eyes soft. "Sounds like you're dealing with a lot right now."

"Detachment's helped me to hold things together my whole life. I don't know how to do this other."

"What about your friendship with Ben Morgan?"

"That's different. That's guy stuff."

"My point is, you've demonstrated that you can get close to someone."

"Not close enough to tell him what's going on now with the new job and all."

"You made a promise to his father, someone whom I believe you care deeply about."

"Life's a bitch."

"Would you like to come again?"

"Do you think I need it?"

"That's for you to decide, not me. From what you've told me, your youth didn't set you up for attachment. It could be useful to explore that a little, maybe try to find ways to let go of some old habits? We could also strategize about your current relationship with Ruthie, if you like?"

"That's my priority right now."

"Of course."

"When's your next free slot?"

"This is always a good time because I don't have regular appointments."

He surprised himself by saying, "How about tomorrow night, same time?"

"That works for me."

"Any advice on how to get through tomorrow?"

Her warm eyes gazed into his. "Your priority is yourself. Take care of yourself. Make your decisions about what's best for you. Maybe do some thinking about what *you* want and what makes you feel at peace and happy."

"That's easy. I feel most at peace in her arms."

Haley grinned. "Well, that's a start. See you tomorrow night."

CHAPTER 42

The Hollywood crew departed Wednesday morning. Tom Harding came by the farm and found her planting Bibb lettuce. "I knew you'd look great in overalls," he said, smiling as she stood up.

"Tom? What are you doing here?"

"Never saw you at dinner last night."

"Yeah, the wedding stuff has kept us pretty busy."

"I just wanted to say goodbye."

"It's been fun spending time with you."

"Wish I could take you back with me."

"My place is here."

"This is not the movie star playboy talking."

"I know, and I'm flattered."

"I don't want you to be flattered. I want you to say you'll be more than friends."

"But I—"

He put up his hands. "No, let's not go there again. Goodbye, beautiful. Hope we meet again." He leaned forward and kissed her dusty cheek.

"Goodbye, Tom. I'll see you at the movies."

He laughed. "I wouldn't recommend it unless you need a sleeping aid."

She hugged him and he walked away.

***

Kyle Morgan arrived midday Wednesday. His brother Ben picked him up. They were sitting with their parents drinking beers when Ruthie pulled in from work. "Hey, brother," she cried, embracing him warmly. "I see you made it for the bachelor party."

"Just hearin' about it. Your girls doin' something with Rose?"

"Yes, dinner at Gracie's. She's reserved the back for us."

"If past bachelor bashes are any indication, I'd guess we'll drive the regular patrons out of the Bulldog quick enough," Ben said.

"How many we talkin'?" Kyle asked.

"Probably ten to twelve. The Morgan brothers, Lang, and Sam's got one friend from Flagstaff. Then there's the stable crew, although Harley's gonna be late. He's been mysteriously busy the past couple of nights. Don't know what the man's up to."

Ruthie listened but said nothing, remembering their encounter with Harley the previous evening. *Whatever he's up to, it's one more thing he's not sharing with me.*

"The pops comin'? Kyle asked.

"Our dad and Spark, but I doubt we'll see Jaybo Dillon."

As if on cue, their parents drove up the driveway. Leonora flew out of the car and came to greet her fifth child. "Oh, sweetie, so good to have you home."

Helen said her hellos and hugged him, his father right behind her. "Hey son, great to have you back." Ben Senior was never so happy as when all his offspring were under one roof, as they'd be for the rehearsal dinner Friday night. He had another reason for being especially glad to see their youngest son. Kyle was just completing his veterinarian residency back east. Who better to hire as resident vet at the new facility than Kyle? Between Kyle and Ned Williams, the animals would be in good hands.

CHAPTER 43

When he walked out of his second hour with Haley, Harley felt more at peace than he had in years. In her gentle, skillful questions he had found some answers. In her deeply attentive presence, he found respite and understanding and they made an appointment for the following night. As he strolled down the sidewalk toward the Bulldog, he realized Haley was giving him tools that might begin to change lifelong habits.

There was a part of him that wanted nothing more than to go home and process his hour with the therapist, but his family won out. By the time he arrived, most people had eaten, so he headed to the bar and ordered a burger and salad. There were appetizers set out on a long table where their group had congregated, and he picked at them as he sipped a Desert Amber.

Ben Morgan patted his friend on the back. "Hey, buddy, good to see you. Everything okay?"

"I guess Maggie told you about Haley?"

"Excuse me?"

"I asked about her therapist. I've been seeing her the past two nights."

"She's good people. Maggie and Beth are crazy about the woman. She really helped us through Maggie's depression after the miscarriage."

"Yeah, she's been helpful. She threw me a lifeline the first night so I'm kind of addicted."

"She's not cheap."

"Worth every penny."

"Hey, Harl," Kyle Morgan said, hugging him. "Good to see the county's most famous wrangler."

"Ha, ha."

As they stood talking, Robbie was drinking shots of tequila with Sam, who looked a little green around the gills. Kyle nudged his older brother. "Stop him, man. Sam's not used to drinking. He's never had Robbie's wooden leg."

"I dare say he'll live," Ben said, nodding to their dad and Spark, who were observing from a table in the corner.

"This is why they hold this shindig tonight," Ben Senior said to his friend. "So the groom can recover before the big day."

Spark laughed. "Why didn't we think of that? I remember a certain groom who almost swooned at the altar after a night of drinkin'."

His friend laughed. "I was swooning cause my bride was so beautiful. Still is."

"That's for damn sure. Her cousin's not too shabby, either."

"You and Helen have been spendin' a lot of time together, my friend."

Spark nodded. "It's been lots of fun. She's a great lady. I'm sorry she'll be leavin' after the wedding."

"We'll get her back."

"I hope so. You know that no one could ever take the place of my Patsy, and I think she feels the same about her recently deceased husband."

"Yes, the second one was a keeper, but the first was and is a bastard."

"He still living?"

"I believe so. They're long divorced. Her recent husband she had known many years ago, but she gave him up for the first, who proved himself a monster as the years went by."

"Haven't we been lucky, my friend."

"The luckiest."

"As I was sayin', I've had the love of my love. Nothing will ever touch that, but I like her, Ben. I really like her. Never thought it was possible."

His friend smiled broadly. "Anything's possible here in the Valley."

"Uh-oh, do you think the groom needs help?" Spark said as they observed Sam keel over a bar stool and fall to the floor.

"Yup, and we're the ones to do it, or supervise, anyway. Kyle, Ben—go get your brother. Time to wrap this up while Rose still has a fiancé."

***

Gracie joined the bride and friends for drinks and dessert following a delicious meal of fresh fish and summer salads. She had made a variety of fruit tarts, light, creamy, and delicious. Since the restaurant was closed, they were all enjoying after-dinner drinks. Rose was a shy, self-deprecating person, so the gathering had reflected her quiet tone. Maggie gave a heartfelt toast to the woman who had changed her life and that of her precious daughter. It had been Rose who first suggested that they consult doctors at the Heavers Clinic about Emma's spinal injury. If not for her, their daughter might still be in a wheelchair today.

As the evening wore on, there was laughter and raucousness, mostly centering around tales of the "Morgan boys" and their friends. All of the Morgan brothers had been ladies' men, all handsome, charming, and full of mischief. Maggie, Beth, and Rose had many high school stories about Ben, Sam, and Harley, but not so many about the others, who were younger. "Sam, was *always* the sensible one!" Rose insisted. "The others were incorrigible. I can just imagine what his wild brothers are doing right now to my sweet husband-to-be."

The party broke up around midnight and Ruthie, the designated driver, got everyone home safely. They had taken one of the Lodge vans to fit everyone. They dropped Martha and Rose off first, then Beth. Sadie was staying at the Lodge. After leaving her there, they took Maggie home. Before she hopped out, she reached forward and patted Ruthie, Helen, and Leonora's shoulders. "That was fun, ladies."

"It certainly was, dear," Leonora said.

"She's a lovely young woman," Helen said as they drove away.

"Yes, she is," Leonora said, remembering how cruel and snobbish she had been when her beloved daughter-in-law had first come into their lives. She hoped that in some ways she had made up for her despicable behavior over the past few years.

Ruthie said goodnight and headed upstairs, her heart heavy and troubled. Again, she had the feeling of Alice in the Looking Glass, wondering whether she'd dreamed about their passionate lovemaking. *And what is he up to every night?*

CHAPTER 44

Leonora handed her youngest a long list of errands.

"I've just gotten back from town, Mama! You know, I have two brothers who are pretty free right now, as opposed to me, who actually has a job. And have you forgotten that it's the Dillons who are giving this wedding? What else could you possibly need?"

"Don't be fresh, Ruthie Ann. You promised me these days, remember? We worked it all out so Robbie could be at the farm. Hope has her hands full with commission work, and Kyle is doing rounds with Ned Williams. Now scoot!"

"Why is it that I'm the only person in this family who is viewed as expendable at my job? What's Ben doing today?"

"Don't be ridiculous. He's on crutches!"

"Doesn't seem to be slowing him down."

"Oh, pish tush, out you go! Shoo! Drop this basket at the stables. Carmela made the crew lunch to thank them for all their extra work this week and over the weekend."

Still fuming at her mother, Ruthie walked through the quiet barn. As she passed through, Harley stepped out of the office.

He smiled. "Hey, what brings you down here?"

She handed him the basket. "At Mother's request, Carmela made lunch for you and the crew, to thank everyone for all the extra work."

"That's kind of her. The guys'll be grateful. Wanta join us?"

He looks different. "Can't. My mother's given me a list a mile long."

He grinned. "Lucky you."

"I'd better get going."

"You been okay?"

She nodded. "You?"

"Yup."

"Alright, then," she said, preparing to go. Abruptly, she turned back to him. "No, I'm not okay. I'm confused, hurt and irritated, if you want to know the truth."

"I'm sorry."

"You should be."

"Ruthie, wait, I do want to talk, to try and explain things, but now's not the right time."

"I get that part. It's never a right time with you! I've gotta go. See you tomorrow night at the rehearsal, if you're even coming?"

"Of course I'm coming," he said softly. "Wouldn't miss it for the world."

She stalked out, fury at her mother forgotten as she now had a new focus for her anger.

***

Harley watched her go, frustrated, but knowing he was handling things the best he could. Haley had suggested that he hold back a little with Ruthie until he really knew how he felt. As Ben had said, they'd been doing this same dance for ten years, so it was familiar, but now everything felt awkward given the white-hot memories of their lovemaking that seared through him. A loner by nature, he was scared to death at the thought of sharing a life with someone, but this…she was different. He needed her like he needed air. Every waking moment his mind, body, and soul ached for her.

***

Thursday was quiet. The Morgan family dined together minus Ben and Maggie, who were meeting Ned in town. Lang and Beth came for a short visit, but Lily was fussy, so they left before dessert. Harley kept his appointment with Haley and made a couple more for the following week. They were a lifeline right now and he found peace in her warm, comfortable consulting room.

When Ruthie went to bed, she checked her cell phone and found a voice mail from Harley, asking if she'd like to have lunch the next day. Shocked, she hit redial. Harley never went out to lunch. *What was this about?*

He answered on the second ring.

"Hey, I got your message," she said. "I can't have lunch. I'm eating with the bridesmaids tomorrow. It's kind of a wedding shower for Rose."

"That's okay. We'll do it another time."

"You working all day tomorrow?"

"Yup, he said."

"Time for a short ride? Maybe an hour or so?"

"I could do that. What time?"

"How about early in the morning? Six thirty? Otherwise, I'll get sucked up in the maw of Leonora's party prep."

"Meet you then," he said. "Thanks."

"See ya," she said softly, clicking off. *Things just get curiouser and curiouser.*

She lay back thinking about the beautiful spot her father and Spark had chosen for the new farm. Their quick trip out to see it had been the only restful hour she'd had all week. She wished she could talk to Harley about it, hear his thoughts and ideas, even if he had kept it a secret like so many others. *Soon,* she sighed, drifting off to sleep. *Soon.*

CHAPTER 45

Ruthie slipped out of the house at six fifteen and drove to the stables. As she headed into the barn, she breathed deeply. Ever since she was a little girl coming for an early morning ride with her dad, this time of day was her favorite. The peace and stillness, the ripe scent of hay, the birds chittering in the rafters, and the soft nickering of the horses. As she reached Jadie's stall, she was surprised to see her gone. She headed out and found Harley talking softly to Pepper, both horses saddled and ready to go.

"Morning," she said.

His eyes met hers, soft and warm. "Morning. We're all set if you are?"

"Let's go," she said, hopping up on Jadie.

"How about the North Horseshoe?" he asked.

"Suits me."

They climbed the ridge and followed the meandering path halfway up, then across until it descended back into a broad, open meadow. As the trail narrowed, she hung back and followed him, marveling at his strong back, wiry frame, and an ass that many a Valley woman had noticed over the years. No one sat on a horse like Harley Langdon. He rarely did competitions any more, but if his name was on a rodeo program, women flocked to the event just to catch a glimpse of him.

The ground leveled and they rode out into the open meadow. As children, they had loved to come this way and stop for a picnic under the enormous cottonwood tree that had, at one time, held two rope swings, one on each side of its thick trunk. Now the ropes were gone, but the tree still provided ample shade for picnics.

As they neared the cottonwood, she drew alongside him. "I wonder if there's a way Polly and Lynn could get the kids out here. Such a great spot. We could put up new swings."

"You sure loved to swing," he said, remembering her red curls flying as she begged to go higher and higher. *I loved to watch her then and now, astride first her ponies and now the pinto.* She'd had Jadie only a couple of years and already they rode as one, which was how he knew with certainty that her former fiancé, Kevin, had to have done something pretty dramatic to cause the steady horse to throw her mistress. Every inch a woman, Ruthie Morgan inhabited a saddle better than any woman he knew. "Wanta stop for a bit? Good a place as any to talk."

In answer, she slipped down and nuzzled Jadie's nose. "Okay." There was challenge in her tone as she settled on a patch of soft grass in the shade. She closed her eyes, leaning back on her arms, breathing deeply. "I love it here."

"Yeah, it's pretty nice," he said, coming to sit beside her.

In her faded blue ranch tee shirt, worn jeans, and boots, she'd never looked more beautiful, Harley thought. She threw off her baseball cap and loosened her hair. Instead of pulling it back in a ponytail again, she set the elastic aside and ran her fingers through her thick auburn curls.

Harley watched, smiling, cock hard as a rock, hidden under the hat in his lap. He knew damn well what she was doing and he loved it. The little girl he'd grown up with was well aware of her sexuality and she knew how to use it. He could have happily watched her all day.

Finally, she opened her eyes, "So, I'm here. You had something you wanted to talk about?"

He nodded. "I think you know I care about you, Ruthie. Very deeply."

"As a little sister. I know."

"Babe, our relationship has gone way beyond brother-sister, don't you think?"

She shrugged. "I thought so, but after the past week, I have no idea. I've wondered if it was just sex to you, getting a last fling before you take off."

"You know that's not true."

"Do I?" She sat up, eyes challenging him.

He put up his hands. "Whoa, okay, this isn't what I wanted to talk about."

"So?"

He recognized that look. She was in full pout mode. "Okay, okay. What I wanted to tell you is that I'm fucked up. I'm pretty much a loner and that's helped me survive. I don't get close to people, you know? I mean, your brother's my best friend, but that's about it."

"But you're part of my family. We all love you. You're close to us."

He nodded. "Your dad's the father I never had and I'm really grateful for that, but I'm talkin' about women, about getting really close. I don't do it or, more accurately, I don't know *how* to do it."

"None of us do."

He shrugged. "Maybe, but when you and I started up, it really freaked me out. It was nothing you did. You've been incredible, but I froze. Seeing you with Tom Harding, I nearly went crazy. That's when I knew I needed help."

"But I've been with other men and you didn't care."

"Oh, I cared, but I knew they wouldn't last."

"Oh, you did, did you?"

He grinned. "I've been seeing a therapist. She's helping me sort through things, but it's a slow process."

"She? When? Who?"

"Haley Alvarez. She's seen me a few nights this past week."

"Maggie's Haley?"

"Yup."

"Is it helping?"

"I think so. At least I'm sleeping better."

"And?"

"I just wanted you to know that I'm trying to be the kind of person who knows how to love you. Not sure I'll get there, but it's not you, babe. It's never been you."

Ruthie sat up and knelt in front of him. "So where does that leave us?" Her arms circled his neck and she drew nearer, her soft breasts pressed against his chest.

"I'm working on that."

"And what about this?" she said, kissing his neck, her lips moving upward. "Wanta tell me what you're hiding under your hat?"

His hands circled her waist as he drew back to gaze down at her. "This may not be a good idea."

"Why not?"

"'Cause you just told me you were worried about the 'just sex' business."

"And you reassured me that it wasn't just sex." She leaned forward, pressing against him, her hand traveling downward, finding his penis straining the fabric of his worn jeans. She began a slow, rhythmic stroking and rubbing, up and down, up and down.

"Jesus Christ, Ruthie, I'm trying to protect you here."

"And what if I don't want protecting?"

"If you keep that up, I'm gonna have to rip your clothes off. You know that."

"Yes, I do," she said, caressing him. She was as aroused as he was and she had no intention of stopping.

She stood up and her jeans and panties fell to the ground, boots kicked aside. Amazed, he gazed up at her glorious body as her tee shirt, too, was thrown aside. She knelt, unzipped and released his cock, then straddled him wearing only her lacy pink bra.

Fingering the straps, he said, "This is what you wear for a trail ride?"

"When I know I'm riding with you, cowboy. You ready for a wild ride?"

He was so ready he was about to explode. "Oh, sweet Jesus, come here babe." He captured her mouth in a deep, hungry kiss, drawing her to him as she swiveled and took him in. He grabbed hold of her ass, pulling her closer.

Ruthie cried out and arched her back, taking him deeper. "Don't stop, cowboy, never, never stop."

As they moved in wild, frenzied unison, she dug her fingers into his back. "More, more, more," she cried, throwing her head back as she thrust against him again and again, lost in a tidal wave of sensation that crested in a blinding, thunderous climax that leaving them both panting and slick with sweat.

As he kissed her softly, she wrapped her legs around him.

"Babe, what the hell was that?"

She smiled. "I'd say it was a lot more than just sex, wouldn't you?"

"Where have you been all my life, you wanton woman?"

She rested her head on his shoulder. "Right in front of you, cowboy."

They sat entwined for a long time until he nibbled her shoulder playfully. "Hey, babe, time to head back."

"I'll bet we have time for a replay?" She began to swivel her hips slowly and languidly at first, then with more insistence.

"Oh, babe."

As she felt him grow hard inside her, she grinned. "You seem to be up for this, cowboy. Am I right?"

"You bet your sweet ass I am," he said, flipping her over, wrapping her legs around his waist and taking her hard and deep.

She arched up to meet him. "Oh, oh, oh, my love" she cried. "Please don't stop, please, please, please!"

His explosive release blotted all reason.

Sated and slick, they lay back and their bodies entwined. They slept briefly until awakened by the buzzing of flies all around them. He kissed her forehead. Then with a low moan he withdrew from her warmth. "Babe, we've really gotta go. I've gotta get back. You, too, I'm guessing?"

"I don't ever want to go back," she said, kissing him.

"We'll come back, I promise."

Dressed and ready to ride, he drew her close for a kiss. "You're using protection, right, babe?"

"Course I am," she lied again. *I'm not about to spoil the moment by admitting I stopped taking the pill four months ago.*

When they returned to the stables, Nick, Jeb, and the college kids were hard at work. "Hey, boss. Mornin', Ruthie," Nick said as they rode by. "Have a nice ride?"

Best ride of my life, Harley grinned at him, pretty sure Parker knew just what kind of ride they'd been on. "Yup, nice morning."

"I've gotta go. Rip, can you cool Jadie down and feed her?" she asked.

He grabbed the pinto's reins. "Sure thing, Ms. Morgan."

As she headed toward the barn, she turned back and waved. "See everyone tonight."

CHAPTER 46

After a flurry of activity, they were rewarded with perfect weather for Sam and Rose's rehearsal dinner. A tent had been erected over the entire terrace of the Big House and six long tables accommodated the guests. In addition to the wedding party and guests, all ranch and winery personnel had been invited. This was always the way at Morgan's Run and the Dillons had followed suit. All were invited tomorrow along with half the town of Saguaro Valley.

Once again Aria, Spark's chef, had joined forces with Carmela and Raoul to bring forth a sumptuous meal. Several grills cooked pork loins, ribs, steaks, and fish. Aria had made all the appetizers, hot and cold, and they included skewers of chicken and beef, scallops wrapped in pea pods, mushrooms stuffed with crab meat and huge platters of cheeses, vegetables, and dips. A dizzying array of Carmela's beautiful salads lined the buffet table as well as baskets of warm, crusty bread. At Sam's request, dessert was ice cream from the Daily Scoop, a variety of flavors and toppings. Carmela had also made two Armadillo groom's cakes with dense red centers and dark chocolate icing.

"Well, you've done it again," Spark said, standing by his friend, drinks in hand. "What a spread."

"Carmela and Aria make a good team, don't they?" Ben Senior said, surveying the scene. "I've eaten so much I'm not sure I can fit in dessert."

"But, we'll give it the old college try, won't we, buddy?"

"Sure will. Let's load up."

"Helen looks pretty tonight, doesn't she?" Spark said as the two made their way toward the buffet.

"She is a handsome woman, for sure," Ben said, smiling at his friend. "She's changed her flight so she can be at our big wingding next Wednesday."

"She told me. I was so pleased. Will make it all the sweeter." He leaned closer, whispering, "You think Leonora's gonna kill you?"

"No, but I'll bet once I make the announcement tonight I won't have a moment's peace till then. She'll be wheedling day and night to find out what we're up to."

"Stay strong, buddy," Spark said, scooping several flavors of ice cream into a bowl.

As the guests drank coffee and finished desserts, several people gave toasts, including Sam's best man and Sadie, Rose's friend. At last Ben Senior stood. "So glad to have everyone here tonight. A huge thanks to our chefs, Aria, Carmela, and Raoul and their hardworking crew. Leonora and I love gathering the folks we love for great food and lively conversation. And, there's nothing better in this whole world than celebrating such a happy occasion as the marriage of our Samuel to the lovely, extraordinary Rose Dillon. We can't wait till tomorrow. How lucky are we that *two* of our kids married into the family of our dear friends and neighbors, Martha and Jaybo Dillon? First our Beth and Lang and now Sam and Rose. To the bride and groom, I offer congratulations and lots of love."

Everyone raised their glasses, clapping and cheering.

Ben Senior put up his hand. "If I could have your attention for one more small announcement, please. While not related to tomorrow's wedding, Spark and I thought since we had you all together, this was the best time to invite one and all to a special picnic next Wednesday. I can't speak for the winery, but if you're working at Foster's or here on the ranch, you are hereby granted a long lunch hour, if you'd like to attend. All are welcome. I'll let my buddy tell you a little more."

Spark rose. "Not much else except logistics. I've arranged for five of those fancy buses—limos, really—to transport us all. If you're wanting to come, please meet at the Lodge parking lot no later than eleven forty-five that day. We'll have everyone back by two."

"You didn't tell us where we're going," Kyle Morgan called out.

"No, we didn't," Spark said, a twinkle in his eye. "That's our little secret. Now let's get back to the focus of tonight. To Rose and Sam, all the best now and always!"

Leonora listened, mouth agape, not saying a thing until her husband and Spark sat down. "What in the world?" she asked.

"Can't a man have a few secrets in life, darlin'?"

"Not when he's married to me, he can't."

Across the table, Ruthie winked at her father, then gazed two tables over as she had been doing all evening to where Harley sat with the stable crew, Ben, Maggie, their kids, and Ned Williams. When their eyes locked, her body temperature rose and she could barely stay in her seat. The primal urge to drag him out of the tent and beg him to make love to her was overwhelming. It was all she could think about, having him fill her up, ravish her, and then turn around and do it again.

"You okay, sis?" Kyle asked.

"Fine, why?"

"Your face is flushed and your breathing is funny."

"Must be the heat," she said, standing. "I'll just get some air."

She wandered off the terrace, rounding the house, out of sight. Within two minutes he was at her side and she leaped into his arms, their kiss hard and deep. "You look incredible tonight, babe," he whispered, his voice ragged with desire.

"I wore this dress for you, cowboy, 'cause the skirt hikes up, and I'm not wearing any panties."

He carried her around to the front of the house, where a stand of lilacs offered cover beside the front porch. Stepping into the shadows, he pressed her against the wall. His lips and tongue traced down the dress's plunging neckline as he pulled the soft fabric aside and took one breast then the other in his mouth. Ravenous, Ruthie arched her back, begging him to take her. "Please Harley, I'll die if you're not inside me. I just know I will," she whispered, her breath coming in panting, short gasps.

"I've never wanted anything or anyone as much as I do you at this moment, babe," he said, unzipping and freeing his stiff, throbbing cock and guiding it into her warm, wet depths, a gentle thrust followed by increasingly forceful, insistent rutting as she urged him on. "Deeper, my love. Please, take me! Harder, faster, rougher!" she begged, stifling the primal cries she longed to scream out.

It seemed as if they could go on forever, lost in a maelstrom of feeling and sensation, the depths of their lovemaking almost unfathomable. When their climax came it was shattering in its intensity. In the aftermath they both fell limp against each other and the wall. As he held her, leaning against her softness, he whispered, "Jesus, now I know you're trying to kill me, Ruthie Morgan."

"I almost died when I saw you come in tonight," she whispered. "I wanted you so badly I almost fainted. It's all I think about."

"Likewise," he said, voice gruff. "I'm just lucky I wore loose khakis 'cause I've had a hard-on since I saw you walk in that dress."

Ruthie laughed, playfully nipping his shoulder. "If it's this bad tonight, what are we gonna do at the wedding?"

"Find lots of shadows and screw the hell out of each other, I guess. That was meant lovingly, by the way. What I feel for you is insane, babe. Just thinking of you gives me a boner. It's literally driving me crazy."

"Any better now?"

"Yeah, but by the time I get home, I'll be horny as hell and craving you like an addict."

She cupped his head in her hands and kissed him sweetly. "I'm sorry, my horny, sizzling-hot cowboy, but we better get back or my mother'll send out a search party."

"Okay. You ready?"

He withdrew and set her down.

Ruthie's legs shook as she searched for her shoes. After finding them, she took thin lacy panties from her pocket.

He grinned. "You sexy little liar."

"I took 'em off under the table before I got up."

"What's the plan here?"

"I'll go through the house and you circle the outside. If we walk in together everyone's sure to know what we've been doing."

"News flash, babe. No matter where we come from, everyone's gonna know what we've been doing."

"Good," she said, kissing him before hurrying around to the front porch and into the house.

CHAPTER 47

Harley slept soundly, but woke before dawn to a knocking on his door. "Who the hell is that?" he muttered, padding across the apartment in boxers and a tee shirt. He opened the door wondering if he was dreaming. "Babe?"

Ruthie stood in the hallway wearing a fluffy white bathroom and flip-flops, a backpack slung over one shoulder. "Aren't you gonna ask me in?"

He stood aside and she waltzed in, throwing the backpack on the sofa.

"What's up?"

"Something under those boxers, for one."

"I told you, just a glimpse of you and this, even at four in the morning."

"It's almost five."

"What are you doing here?"

"Should I go?"

"No, of course not. What's with the bathrobe?"

"It seemed easiest," she said, untying the belt and letting the robe slip off her shoulders to the floor, revealing her naked, rosy body.

"Oh, my God, you're beautiful, babe. Come here." He crossed the distance between them and kissed her, his hands all over her, caressing, cupping her breasts, licking and sucking. Ruthie threw her head back, already lost in a blur of sensation, as he lifted her and carried her into the bedroom.

Laying her down, he gently spread her legs, his hands, fingers, and tongue moving up her thighs to her moist wetness. His tongue found her sweet center, teasing and stroking her clit to a blinding orgasm. "Oh, Harley, I love…I need… Oh, God, oh God!" she cried, so lost in sensation that she was delirious.

When it was over, she lay still, spent and sated, his head resting on her tummy. "Not fair," she said. "You know how much I want you."

"Do I look like I'm going anywhere?"

She grinned, rolled over, and sat up. "My turn, then," she said, as her hands caressed his erect penis. "Can't let this beautiful thing go to waste." She took him into her mouth, tongue and lips stroking, an agonizing rhythm that had him panting and groaning in seconds.

"Jesus, babe," he said, lost in an explosive orgasm. As his body settled, she sat up, smiling down at him.

"That was amazing babe. Thank you," he said as she straddled him.

"*You* are amazing, cowboy. Got anything left for one last ride?"

"You bet your sweet ass. Come here." Hands on her hips, he moved her up and down on him, back and forth as he grew hard underneath her moist, warm mound. "You gonna do the honors, or shall I?"

Without a word, she rose and guided him in, settling down and taking him as she swayed and swiveled, then began slow, languid thrusts that soon grew more frantic. He reached up and cupped her breasts as she rode him hard. Then all at once, his arm went round her back and he flipped her underneath him. "You're mine now, babe. You want more?"

"You know I do!" She smiled, panting as they crashed together again and again, bringing each other to heights of pleasure beyond reason and thought. In the final moment, their lips found each other and tongues twined as he pounded into her and she arched to take him still deeper.

When they finally lay spent in each other's arms, he kissed her softly. "You are incredible, Ruthie Morgan."

"I love you," she murmured, as her eyes closed and she drifted off to sleep.

They woke at seven and she hopped up and into the shower. Before he could follow her, she was out and dressed in clothes she'd brought in the backpack. As he came out to the living room, she was stuffing the bathrobe and flip-flops into her bag. Now dressed in jeans, a tee shirt, and boots, she said, "Gotta run, sorry. I promised Beth I'd do a couple of things at the farm this morning."

"No problem," he said sleepily. "You want breakfast?"

"Thanks, but I'll grab a bagel and coffee at the café." She paused and stared at him, then crossed the room for one last kiss. "You look pretty cute in those boxers, cowboy."

"Damn, and I was going for hot."

"That, too. See you tonight!"

As the door closed behind her, he shook his head. *What in the hell was that? And how the hell am I gonna explain it to Haley this morning?*

Chapter 48

"It's like she's heroin and I'm addicted. I've never been addicted to anything or anyone in my life."

Haley smiled at him. "This is a big change from the Harley I met a week ago. I'm wondering if this addiction, or perhaps irresistible attraction, may signal you opening up and beginning to let someone in."

"I mean, I've lived around the woman for most of my life. I've always cared for her and her welfare, but nothing like this. All I have to do is catch sight of her and I can't breathe. Not to mention the reaction in other parts of my anatomy."

"Could it be love?"

"That's why I came to see you in the first place. What do you think?"

"It would be better if you figure that out yourself. I do think it's interesting that these addiction feelings seem to have arisen since you and I began these sessions. It's like you've given yourself permission to feel and sense in ways you closed off in the past."

"Do you think I closed off lust or love?"

She smiled.

"You're not gonna answer that, are you?"

"Sorry. Aside from the lust, can you put into words how you feel about Ruthie?"

"I'm crazy about her."

"Crazy in love or crazy with lust?"

"Both."

"Have you told her that you love her?"

"Not in so many words. Maybe sort of."

"Sort of enough that she heard and understood you?"

"Honestly, probably not."

"Can you say why?"

"I guess it's fear of leading her on?"

"So it's just sex?"

"Of course not."

"Then why let her go on thinking it's just sex?"

Green eyes that usually met hers so directly looked away. He sat silent and uncomfortable for several minutes. Finally, she said, "Harley?"

He shrugged. "I'm trying to figure it out. I mean, Ruthie's loved me since I can remember and I've always loved her in a brother-sister kind of way. That was easy. This is more complicated."

Haley nodded. "Affairs of the heart between men and women are, indeed, very different."

"More permanent?"

"Maybe, but is it permanence and commitment what's holding you back?"

"Maybe. To be honest, it feels more like fear. That's what I've been sitting here thinking, how afraid I am."

"Of?"

"Loving someone."

"Can you think why? Are you afraid being hurt?"

He smiled. "No."

"Then what about love scares you?"

"The only thing I can come up with is fear of failure and not being good enough for her."

"Where does that come from, do you think?"

"Well, she's a Morgan, for Christ's sake, and I'm just a cowboy from humble beginnings."

"Hmm…" Haley said, watching him.

"Is there something behind that 'hmm'?"

"The whole 'she's too high and mighty for humble old me' thing doesn't seem to ring true, especially considering the position Ben Senior has offered you."

"I don't know how to treat a woman."

"Is this a problem?"

"Well, yeah."

"Does Ruthie know how to treat a man?"

"I guess. Certainly when it comes to sex."

"And you're inadequate there?"

"I don't think so," he said, blushing slightly, a grin on his handsome face.

"Then when are you inadequate?"

"I don't know. I've never been there."

"What's the worst that could happen?"

"She could know the real me."

Haley smiled. "Is that so bad?"

He shrugged.

"Our time's up and I have someone coming."

"Oh, sure, of course."

"Harley, wait. I don't want to leave you there. What I wanted to say is—I'd bet the ranch that Ruthie Morgan already knows the real you and she loves you just the way you are. We think we hide ourselves from others, but most of the time we're right there, warts and all."

He put on his hat, tipping it. "Thanks, Haley. See you tonight."

She smiled back at him. *Nothing like a man in a Stetson, particularly this one.* "Yes, looking forward to it."

CHAPTER 49

"Hey, where is everyone?" Ruthie called as she stepped into the Dillon's house.

"Up here!" Beth said, waving from the upstairs bannister.

"Are we the only two here?"

"And Sadie," Beth whispered. "Rose didn't want any of this, so she's hiding in her room, refusing to let the stylist near her."

"Where's Maggie?"

"She's doing her own hair and makeup at home. Too complicated with the kids and camp opening tomorrow."

"Where my brother? Couldn't he take them?"

"He's supervising things at camp, probably doing too much."

"Hi, girls!" Martha said. "Please convince my daughter to at least have a touch of makeup. I love what Katrina's done for me." She breezed by, headed downstairs.

They knocked at Rose's door and heard her voice uncharacteristically shrill. "If that's you, Mother—go away!"

"It's Beth and Ruthie," Beth said.

The door opened almost immediately to reveal a distraught bride, her demeanor like a caged animal. "Sorry, ladies, it's my mother. She's gone completely crazy over this wedding. I told Sam we should elope or just have the family at a restaurant. The minute we agreed to the vineyard, we lost all control!"

"The tent looks really pretty," Ruthie said, coming to sit next to her almost-sister-in-law.

"Oh, it all looks gorgeous. Mother and Jon have gone wild. He brought in a whole crew from Laguna Beach—"food people," he calls them. Sam's so lucky he moved to the Big House two days ago." Jon Wilson was the Dillon's chef, who had migrated to the Valley from Laguna Beach five years ago. He now resided in the beautiful apartment Martha decorated for him above the garages.

"Want us to call Sam?" Beth asked. "Maybe a little time with him would feel good right about now? Lang always calms me down."

"I'll survive, I'm sure. My dad's insisting on walking me down the aisle, but we'll all be relieved when we get to the altar."

An alcoholic of many years, Jaybo Dillon often began drinking in the early afternoon. Ill health the past few years had slowed him down, but his behavior was still erratic and unpredictable.

"Lang's all set to step in, if needed," Beth said, patting her hand. "Now I think I'll let Katrina apply a little light makeup and do something with this limp, dull hair. Any other takers?"

"I'm game," Ruthie said. "What about you, Rose?"

"What do you both think? Should I let her do my hair or face?" she asked, her lovely hazel eyes pleading.

Both sisters stepped back, gazing at her. Rose's was a natural beauty, with an understated, quiet loveliness that needed little adornment. It was obvious to both sisters why Sam loved her. She was smart, kind, and beautiful inside and out. At the moment, her shoulder-length ash-blond hair hung limply.

"Hmm," Ruthie said. "Didn't Maggie say they'd made a garland of flowers for Emma's hair?"

"Yes, they dropped off flowers here and sent Maggie's, Emma's, and the boys' over there. We can cover ourselves in blooms if we want."

Ruthie smiled. "I was thinking the bridesmaids could have Katrina weave some flowers in our hair and either do the same for you or make you a garland since you're not wearing a veil, right?"

Rose nodded. "I think Sam would like the flowers. Not a garland, though."

"Well, let's have Katrina come in and we'll each supervise what she does to the others and give suggestions. How about that?"

Rose's face brightened, and she said, "I am so lucky to have you both as sisters. Thank you!"

As Rose went to summon Katrina, Beth said, "How was everything at the farm?"

"Fine. The guys've got things covered. One man'll stay on and the rest are planning to come tonight. They drew straws."

"They're the best. By the way, Mother wanted to know why you had to be at the farm so early. Before dawn, according to her."

"I took a little detour," Ruthie said, blushing.

"Uh-huh? Wouldn't be to a certain wrangler's condo, would it?"

"Oh, gosh, Beth, I have to tell someone! It's been incredible. We can't get enough of each other."

"For two people who've been at odds for most of our growing up, this is an about-face. What brought about this dramatic change?"

"I don't know, but I'm enjoying the ride."

"Are you being careful?"

"Protection, you mean?"

"Well, that, but I was really talking about your heart."

"You know I've loved him for so long. I'll take him any way I can get him."

"Get who?" Rose said, coming in, Katrina in her wake.

Ruthie laughed. "Not on your wedding day, dearie. I promise we'll have the X-rated girl talk after the honeymoon."

Beth gave her sister a look. "Yes, and I suppose Sam and Rose have been living in separate bedrooms in Maryland." Then, remembering the stylist who stood with her basket, waiting, she said, "Don't mind us, Katrina. Let's get started!"

CHAPTER 50

"Your dress is perfect," Helen said. "Martha looks beautiful, too." Ben Senior, Leonora, and Helen Winthrop stood talking to Jaybo Dillon as guests drifted onto the Dillons' terrace for the ceremony. Leonora did indeed look lovely in a floor-length peach gown with a matching beaded jacket.

"Thanks, sweetie. Martha and I bought them together. Your dress is perfect, too."

Helen laughed. "Not sure when I'll ever wear it again, but I'm so glad you suggested I visit Gabriela. She does have the magic touch."

Relieved his friend and neighbor was sober and looking hearty, Ben Senior patted Jaybo's shoulder. "Nora and I just passed through the house. Not a prettier collection of women for a hundred miles."

"And Amy and Maggie aren't even here yet. Where are they, do you suppose?" Leonora asked.

"Plenty of time, darlin'," her husband said. "Here comes the stable crew." He waved to Harley, Nick, Rip, and Sandy, and the townspeople who were passing by.

"Your Mr. Langdon is a handsome man, isn't he?" Helen whispered to Leonora.

"Too handsome for his own good," her cousin said.

"Now, honey, Harley's family."

"Not for much longer," she said, watching him. Truth was, she'd miss her adopted son, and he did look gorgeous today in his groomsman suit of dark blue, tie matching the bridesmaids' dresses. *If he breaks my little girl's heart, I'm going to kill him.*

A beautiful white tent festooned with fresh flowers and bordered by potted plants, all draped with twinkly lights, stretched from the terrace to the vineyard barn. The huge barn, where they processed the wines in rows of barrels, also had a commercial kitchen where Jon Wilson and his crew had set up shop. There were two bars at either end of the tent and food stations at all four corners. Lang had been put in charge of keeping his father away from the bars. The father-son relationship had soured years ago and was still fragile at best, but for his sister's and mother's sakes, he tried to stay civil.

Neecy, the Dillons' housekeeper, made sure all groomsmen and the fathers had their boutonnieres of desert roses set on dark greenery. They looked stunning on the dark blue suits.

"Look at them," Leonora said as they watched the groomsmen ushering people to their seats. "The boutonnieres are perfect, aren't they? Martha has exquisite taste. And, could they be any more handsome? All of them!"

"Don't forget your handsome husband," Helen said, smiling.

"Never. He's in a league all by himself," she said as the two women watched Ben Senior greeting people. "He's in his glory tonight."

When everyone was seated, the music shifted and Ben walked Leonora down the aisle while his father escorted Helen. Lang then brought Martha to her seat and the groomsmen all came forward to stand to the side of the groom. Sam Morgan, tall with the build of the long-distance runner he was, stood calmly, his best man, brother Ben Morgan, crutches hidden, beside him. People often called the dark-haired brothers clones, even though Ben was broader than Sam. Kyle, too, had dark hair, but was much shorter than his older siblings. With his light hair and eyes, Robbie favored his beautiful mother. The tallest groomsman, Harley, stood at the end of the row, his expression calm. To his right, Pete Carroll, Sam's college roommate, stood, a sharp contrast to the others with his carrot-red hair and freckled face.

The music shifted again and Emma came first, strewing pink rose petals from her tiny white basket. She was dressed in white, and her sash was of the same fabric as the bridesmaids' dresses. She looked adorable with a garland of flowers crowning her dark brown, curly hair. When she reached the front, she winked at her father, then went to sit with her grandparents in the front row. Behind her came baby Ben with a small silver box. It took some coaxing to get him down the long aisle, but when he finally reached the wedding party, his father scooped him up in his arms.

Next came the bridesmaids. Maggie wore an off-the-shoulder dress similar to Ruthie's, her glorious cleavage on full display. Like the others, she had flowers in her hair. Amy Foster-Barnes and Beth followed in more simple, looser sheaths. Then it was Ruthie's turn. When Harley spied her, his carefully composed demeanor collapsed and his mouth hung open.

Leonora poked her husband and whispered, "Look at our stable manager. Tell me he isn't as crazy about her as she is him."

Ben Senior grinned, hugging her to him.

Sadie Thomas, Rose's maid of honor, came last, her short, curvaceous figure in a style similar to Maggie's and Ruthie's dresses. Then the music shifted to the Wedding March and Rose and her father appeared from the house. She wore a simple sleeveless gown trimmed with delicate lace, flowers woven into her hair, which Katrina had curled slightly so that it framed her lovely face. When Sam saw her, every moment of the stylist's fussing had been worth it. His eyes shone with love and admiration.

"Oh, honey," Leonora whispered. "Another one of our darlings has found true love. Aren't we lucky?"

He kissed the top of her head. "The luckiest."

CHAPTER 51

Following a cocktail hour with all manner of hot and cold appetizers, Jon and his crew set up the four food stations—one with fish, another beef, pork, and chicken, a third with pasta, and the fourth with an array of beautiful seasonal vegetable dishes and salads. Servers ready stood at each station.

As Leonora and her cousin moved along the vegetable station, Helen said, "I've never seen so much food in my life."

"That's 'cause you've never experienced a ranch wedding. That's not to say that Jon and his staff haven't outdone themselves. They have. I love all the California touches, too."

"Hey, ladies," Spark said, putting his full plate out to the server for a small serving of salad, all that could fit beside his huge pile of meat. "What a night. Bride looks beautiful. What a spread."

"Where're you sitting?"

"With Amy, Jeb, and my grandson."

"Come sit with us, darlin'," Leonora said. "The young people won't miss you."

He laughed. "I expect you're right about that. Let me check in with them. Save me a seat if you can."

"Your buddy's got one with your name on it already."

One of the few requests Martha honored was Rose and Sam's insistence that guests should choose their own seats. So aside from the bridal party, people sat wherever they chose.

Harley brought his plate of mostly vegetables and salad to sit next to Kyle Morgan. Of the other Morgan brothers, he knew Kyle the best since he often spent time at the stables when home.

"Hey, Harley, looking good. I hear we're losing you to sunny California."

He shrugged, hating to continue the lie when they'd all learn the truth soon enough.

"How's the veterinary business going?"

"Great. I complete my residency in three months and I'll be looking for a job. Not sure where I want to be. I thought New England would be where I'd settle, but this year I've been missing the Valley, you know?"

"They sure need vets out here. Ned's really all they've got and he won't operate."

"They must have a resident vet up there in Napa."

"Two."

"Don't s'pose either of them hinted that they might be leaving? Napa would be a great place to start out."

"It's not the Valley, though."

"No place is. Hey, didn't my baby sister grow up this year?"

Harley smiled, giving him a look.

"She still sweet on you?"

He hesitated, then said, "Actually, we've been seeing each other a little now that's she's grown up."

"You're kidding?"

"Nope."

Kyle patted him on the back. "Well, it's about time, buddy. Do my folks know?"

"You'd have to ask your sister. I haven't discussed it with them."

"Hey, doesn't Rose look happy? She's good for Sam," Kyle said as the bride and groom took to the floor for their first dance.

CHAPTER 52

"Would you look at Helen and Spark?" Leonora said, watching their dear friend whirl her cousin around the dance floor.

Ben Senior put his arm around his wife, pulling her closer. "He's sweet on her, you know."

"That's wonderful! Patsy would want him to be happy."

"Hope he doesn't move back East."

"Don't be ridiculous. Why would anyone choose to leave here?"

"It happens, darlin'."

"If you're referring to that turncoat Harley Langdon, I'm mad at him."

"Look like he's headed to ask our baby to dance."

"If he breaks her heart, you must promise me you'll shoot him."

Ben laughed. "Oh, boy, here's comes the dirty dancing. This younger generation sure knows how to move."

"And your eldest son and Maggie are some of the worst offenders. He supposed to be on crutches, not making love on the dance floor. Just look at them, and with their children present!"

"Isn't it marvelous! Reminds me of us once upon a time."

Leonora elbowed him, smiling. "Oh, pish tush!"

Valley events usually had many more men than women, so Harley had watched Ruthie dancing with men from town, ranch workers, her brothers, and Pete Carroll, waiting for a break in the action. Finally, she stepped off the dance floor to cool off and grab a drink, and he came to her side before someone else could snatch her up.

"Too tired for another?" he asked, extending his hand.

"I've been wondering when you'd ask me."

"Pretty tough with all these cowboys."

The music shifted to Bob Seger and they were off. Harley was an excellent dancer, and they moved in perfect synchrony. Ben nudged Maggie. "That's what I call love."

"Except that he's leaving soon."

"Maybe Shortcake'll go with him?"

"You think so?"

"Stranger things have happened."

The next dance was slow as the band played a moody rendition of Percy Sledge's "When a Man Loves a Woman." Harley pulled her close and knew he'd lost it, grateful again for loose slacks. Her breath on his neck was enough to send him right over the edge.

Ruthie rubbed against him, whispering, "Hey, cowboy, you better stay pressed against me, or everyone's gonna know how much you want me. I am going crazy. Do you have any idea how hot I am?" She began nibbling his ear and kissing his neck.

"Cut that out or I'll be compelled to fuck you right here on this dance floor."

"Wouldn't that be interesting," she purred, rubbing her body up and down, back and forth over his rock hard cock.

Across the dance floor, Ben and Robbie Morgan stood with their parents. "Would you look at our baby sister?" Robbie said. "She's practically you-know-whating old Harl on the dance floor."

"Don't be crude, Robbie!" his mother said, frowning at him.

"He's right, Mom," her son Ben said, laughing. "Your little girl has certainly grown up."

Leonora turned to her husband. "Remember what I said. I wasn't kidding about the gun, you know."

"Come on, sweetie. Let's see if you and I can show 'em how it's done!"

When the dance ended, Ruthie and Harley were both delirious with desire. Ruthie wrapped her arms around his neck and whispered, "You know what I want?"

"What, babe?"

"I want is to find a soft hay bale or two in that fancy barn of Jaybo's, or a boulder, wine barrel, whatever. Then I want to lean over and pull up my skirt so you can fuck the daylights out of me. How about that? Think it'll quench this fire?"

"I don't know, but why the hell are we still in this tent?" he growled, taking her hand.

Chapter 53

Their departure did not escape the notice of her parents. "That's trouble, I'm telling you," Leonora said. "And if he thinks he's taking our baby to Napa Valley, he has another think coming."

"Now honey, you forget, Sam and Kyle are all across the country. Means we raised 'em right, to follow their dreams and have their own lives."

"Are you seriously going to stand there and tell me that Ruthie Ann's dreams are not in this Valley? Men are hopeless!"

Ben Senior winked at his son Ben, who whispered. "I know he says he's going, but when push comes to shove, I'll bet the ranch Harley can't leave, either."

His father stared at him in surprise, wondering if Harley had spilled the beans.

"Hey, Dad, what's the matter?"

Ben Senior patted is son's shoulder. "Nothin', son. You were doing pretty good out on that dance floor with the leg."

"Maggie's a strong woman and I hold on tight."

***

It was a clear, starry night, a half moon lighting their way as they strolled across the Vineyard lawn arm in arm, his hand moving up and down her back. "Where to, babe? You know this place better than I do."

"This way," she said, taking his hand and leading him toward another barn beyond the winery. The night was clear and the herd grazed in the meadow to the west, so the barn was empty. The pungent smell of fresh hay greeted them at the door and darkness blanketed the cavernous space, punctuated by shafts of moonlight from the stall windows.

"Not sure I'm horny enough to hop on a pile of cow dung."

"These are prize Angus steers, cowboy."

"Not even on prize Angus shit, babe."

"Come on," she said, leading the way to a ladder. They climbed to a broad, open hayloft, lit by a row of windows along both sides. "We used to play up here as kids." She turned to him, eyes luminous in the moonlight.

"Ruthie, I have something I want to say."

"Not now. Kiss me, please."

He drew her to him, kissing her deeply, endeavoring to show her what he hadn't had time to say, that he loved her beyond all reason and couldn't live without her another day. The physical part had put him over the edge, but it happened because he had finally cracked open his heart.

She returned his kiss, her hands moving down to caress him. "You remember what I said, cowboy? What I wanted?"

"Babe, I remember everything you say," he said huskily, afraid he couldn't hold on much longer. He cupped her breasts, squeezing and teasing as his lips moved down her slender neck, her lemony scent arousing him more.

"Then take me now, please, take me hard. I want your hard, magical cock inside me more than I've ever wanted anything in my life." She took his hand and guided it under her skirt so he could feel her slick, warm wetness. "See?"

He slipped the loose collar of her dress down to take first one, then the other breast in his mouth, licking, sucking, and driving her wild with longing. "Have you been wet like that all night?"

"You mean ready for you or not wearing underwear?" she asked, unzipping his fly, releasing him, hands caressing his penis, breathlessly anticipating the moments ahead.

"Both."

"I slipped my panties off as we came into the barn and I've been ready for you since I first caught sight of you. Don't make me wait any longer. Take me, take me, take me."

He gazed down at her and whispered, "My beautiful love."

He kissed her softly and her body melted into him, her knees shaking. Suddenly, strong hands grabbed her tiny waist and he flipped her, settling her over a stack of hay bales. As he lifted her skirt, he whispered in her ear, "You sure about this, sweetheart?"

"Yes," she said softly.

"Okay, love," he said, voice husky as he reared and slammed into her.

The force took her breath away and she gasped, "Oh, oh, oh!"

He paused. "Did I hurt you?"

She lifted herself on tiptoes, beckoning him. "Don't stop, please! I want more. More and more and more!"

"Jesus, Ruthie, I love you," he said as he rutted almost unconsciously into a sea of sensation. Minutes stretched on as primal forces and a longing that seared his soul drove his frenzied thrusts. When she cried out, her orgasm shaking her body, he let go as well, collapsing on top of her, arms slipping around to cradle her.

Carefully he moved them to rest on their sides, making sure to stay deep within her. As they lay nestled together, he kissed the back of her neck. "You okay, babe?"

"More than okay," she replied, her voice tiny and soft. "You said you love me."

"Yes, I did," he said, nuzzling her neck. "You wouldn't let me say it before, but it just slipped out."

"I'm glad it did."

"You sure you're okay? That was pretty rough."

"Yes, it was, but I loved it. Also, fair warning—you're kissing one of the most erogenous places on my body and I'm getting hot all over again." To emphasize her point, she squeezed him from deep inside her.

"Good to know about that erogenous spot," he said, kissing and licking her there. "I might be able to do something about that."

Cock already hard, he slowly moved in and out of her, their lovemaking gentle. They lay on their sides, and his hands moved up and down her body, caressing her, loving her, all the while thrusting deeper as she arched back to meet him. As they moved toward climax, she cried out, a sound that touched his heart as he let go.

***

The rest of the night was a blur of goodbyes as Sam and Rose headed off for two days in Santa Fe. When they returned to the tent, Ruthie played with her nieces and nephews. As Harley moved to go, Ben Morgan caught up with him. "Hey, buddy, have a nice stroll in the moonlight?"

Harley grinned. "Something like that. And, don't start."

"Just wondering with all that hay on your fancy blue suit and more than a few stalks stickin' out of my baby sister's hair. Am I gonna have to rally my brothers to defend her honor?"

"What about *my* honor?"

Ben laughed. "Well, there's that, too. I hafta warn you, Leonora's already given my dad his marching orders. If you break her heart, he has to shoot you."

"Night, buddy. For what it's worth, your sister's more than capable of defending her own honor."

CHAPTER 54

Monday morning, Ruthie woke up nauseous for the second day in a row. She had attributed the previous day's ill feeling to the late wedding night and the intensity of their lovemaking. *An almost out-of-body experience*, she mused, nibbling at dry toast.

Her mother came in to the dining room, giving her a hard look. "Mornin' darlin'. You okay? You look a little green around the gills and you were draggin' around all day yesterday. Maybe you should see the doctor?"

After spending the entire Sunday day and night with her mother's henpecking, she was in no mood for more. "Gotta run, Mama. You and Helen have a fun day."

"Now wait a minute," Leonora called to her retreating back.

"Bye, Mama." she waved over her shoulder and disappeared into the kitchen.

***

Still dragging at three, Ruthie gave in to the inevitable and told Beth she was knocking off early. She drove into town and parked outside the pharmacy. Fortunately, she did not recognize the woman behind the register who slid the box across the counter. "That'll be fourteen ninety-eight," she said brightly. As she handed Ruthie her change, she said, "Good luck!"

Outside, she gazed around. There was no way she could take the test at home. She pulled out her cell and called the Big House. Carmela answered.

"Hey, Carm, I've just met up with some friends in town, so I won't be back for dinner. Can you let my parents know?"

"Of course," the housekeeper said and they rang off.

Ruthie walked the three blocks to Gracie's, which was mercifully almost empty before the dinner rush. "Hey, Gracie," she called as the owner served two strangers at the counter.

The owner waved. "Be right over, doll!" she said, then disappeared into the kitchen. A few minutes later, she reappeared, her usually stained apron relatively clean and only a few crumbs in her short, frizzy salt and pepper hair. "What can I get you, sweetie?"

She suddenly realized she wasn't the least bit hungry. "What kind of soup do you have tonight?"

"Chili, vegetable beef, cream of mushroom, and chicken and rice. All made today."

Ruthie gazed at the owner, who was like an eccentric, kindly aunt to most of the Valley's residents. "Can I have a bowl of the chicken and rice, some crackers, and a Coke, please?"

"You feelin' okay, pumpkin? You look a little peaked."

She gave her a weary smile. "Just tired. It's been a long day."

"Well, then, I better get that soup right out to you. How 'bout a fresh muffin to go with it? I've got blueberry, cranberry, and some nice warm corn muffins."

"Thanks, Gracie, but the soup'll be fine."

When the owner disappeared, she peeked into her purse at the box, but decided it would be best to eat first. Gracie appeared almost instantly with the soup, her soda, and several packets of various kinds of crackers. "Enjoy, pumpkin."

The soup with its rich broth and fresh vegetables was just what she needed. Between it and the soda and crackers, she was feeling a bit better when she went to pay the check. Gracie waved her money away with, "Nope, on me. You barely ate a thing. Now scoot. A good night's sleep is what you need, baby."

Clearly the diner owner still regarded her as a ten-year-old. *If you only knew, Gracie. Time to face the music.*

She slipped into the diner bathroom and unwrapped the box, not surprised when several minutes later the stick showed a clear blue vertical line. She hadn't really needed it to confirm what a stupid little fool she'd been. On top of the fact that she had taken no precautions, she had lied to Harley. He had told her he loved her Saturday night. *What will he do now? Run for the hills, that's what.*

CHAPTER 55

"Hey, buddy, I'm taking off. Gotta pick up the kids and get down to camp for dinner." Ben Morgan said as the two men finished going over the rest of the week's chores.

Harley gazed over at him. "Don't you ever stop?"

Even on crutches, Ben was a whirlwind of activity. He spent every day shuttling between the barn, the Lodge, and the camp and never seemed to tire. His physical limitations meant that he took a more supervisory role in all settings, and often had to be reminded to "not be so bossy," according to his wife.

"Don't want moss growin' over my ankles."

"Fat chance of that. Besides, you can always beat it down with your crutches, which you don't appear to be using."

"You headin' home? Cause you're welcome to join us for beans and hot dogs at the campfire circle."

"Thanks, but I've got an appointment with Haley later."

"It helping?"

"Far as I can tell. I'm no expert, but she's a good listener."

"You know, you could just ask Ruthie out, then propose. Anything to put us all out of our misery. My mother says she's been moping about for the last two days."

"Oh?"

"Exactly. See ya."

On the off chance she'd catch him, Ruthie drove by the stables on her way home. *Better to get it over with since everyone knows I've always been Miss Impulsive and a hopeless flibbertigibbet!* She spied her brother's Rover as he turned up the road to the Cottage, breathing a sigh of relief that she had missed nosey Parker. Harley's truck was the only vehicle in the lot. She found him in the office, bent over his paperwork.

"Hey," she said softly, stepping into the cluttered room and closing the door.

He stood, eyes full of concern. "Hey, are you okay? Ben says you've been unwell. I was hoping to see you yesterday."

She rolled her eyes. "I was on a death march with my mother and Helen. We went to the Desert Museum, then shopping in Tucson. I mean, I love Helen, and the museum's one of my favorite places, but my mother drives me crazy. Sorry, I meant to call."

He smiled softly as he ran his hands up and down her arms. "No problem, babe. I could have called you, too, you know.'"

"Ben says it's been crazy over here."

"Pretty much."

"You alone?"

"Yup, about to head out. What's up?"

"I have two things I need to tell you."

"Oh?"

"Maybe we better sit down."

"But not before I do this," he said, kissing her softly. "I've missed you, babe."

"Me, too."

The kiss deepened, and his lips trailed down her neck. "And I'll also want to do this," he said as he slipped her dirty tee shirt over her head, hands fondling her glorious breasts. "And this," he continued, unfastening her bra and sliding it off.

"Harley, I'm filthy dirty. I probably smell awful."

"You smell incredible, babe," he said. "if anyone smells gamey, it's me."

"I love your smell," she whispered, responding to his kisses and the feeling of him, hard and aroused, tickling her belly.

"In that case, I'll want to do this," he growled, his hand slipping down her jeans and panties, fingers gliding into her warm, moist folds.

He gazed down at her, grinning, and she smiled despite her fear of what her revelation would do to their relationship.

"What else you gonna do, cowboy?"

"How 'bout this?" he said, unbuttoning her jeans and sliding them down along with her panties. As Ruthie kicked off her boots, then the rest, he pulled his tee shirt over his head and unbuttoned his jeans. As she watched, he checked that the door was latched, placed a wooden chair in the center of the room and sat.

"Then I'll want to ask the love of my life to come here and wrap her gorgeous legs around me." When she stood in front of him, he lifted her in one fluid motion and set her down on his cock, holding her aloft, entering her slowly, her exquisite tightness enveloping him.

She arched her back, giving herself to him, taking him deeper as he sucked and licked her breasts. Finally, she threw herself onto to him, each thrust bringing him in, deeper and fuller. "I love you so much," she cried as they rode the crest of an explosive orgasm.

"Babe," he whispered, all thought obliterated as they reached new heights of sensation.

After, she lay limp in his arms.

"Am I too heavy?" she whispered as he kissed her softly.

"Never."

You just wait, she thought, suddenly remembering the reason for her visit. "Harley, I can't stay long."

"Me, neither, although I'd sure like to take you home with me. I've got an appointment with Haley. You are welcome to come over and use the apartment. Stay overnight?"

"Thanks, but I can't. We've got a really early morning tomorrow. Two of our biggest buyers are coming in for a pickup at seven."

"There's always tomorrow night, sweetheart. Let's get you dressed." Gently, his strong arms lifted her to stand and he began gathering her clothes, dressing her as if she was a child. When he finished, he sat her down, kissing her again before gathering his own things. When they were both dressed, he pulled up another chair to sit in front of her, taking her hands. "So, what's up?"

"I have two things, really, so I'll start with the easiest. I know about the thoroughbred farm. Dad told me when I was having a meltdown over you and me. He took me out there the other day. It's going to be incredible. He made me promise I wouldn't say anything, even to you, but I feel bad keeping things from you, so there it is."

"I did the same thing, babe."

"Yes, but Dad's your boss and I would never expect you to betray your promise to him."

He squeezed her hands. "Well, I'm glad you know."

"The other thing is, well… let me first say I'm glad you're sitting down. Let me also say in advance that I'm really sorry. I've been irresponsible all my life and that hasn't changed. All the PR about me is true. I know my brothers call me a spoiled brat and they're right, but you don't deserve this."

His green eyes stared at her, full of concern. "Okay, babe, now you're scaring me. What's wrong?"

"I'm pregnant."

"But, I thought you said—"

"I know, I lied, or sort half lied since I thought I was safe. You know, at the times in my cycle when we had sex."

He grinned, the laconic, gorgeous Harley Langdon grin that had made many a woman swoon. "From my calculations, I'd say we've pretty much covered the range of your cycle, babe."

"This is not funny!"

"No, it's great. A little surprising, but great. There's no one I'd rather have a baby with than you, sweetheart."

"But what will Willow think?"

"She probably think—how cool to have a baby brother or sister."

Tears rolled down Ruthie's cheeks. "You're not mad?"

"No, baby, I'm not mad. We'll figure this out. It's getting late. I can call Haley and cancel?"

"No, absolutely not! Besides, you'll have lots to talk about with this news!"

"Hey, come here," he said, pulling her to sit on his lap. "It's gonna be fine, baby. You'll see."

CHAPTER 56

Already exhausted from the emotions of the previous day, a poor night's sleep, and a very early rising, Ruthie stood with Beth, watching the last truckload of produce roll down the farm drive. Her sister turned to her. "Hey, I'm gonna take a quick drive to the Cottage to have lunch with Lily. Wanta come? Lang made our lunches and he always packs enough for ten."

"Thanks, but I think I'll stay here. I might even lie on the back porch and close my eyes."

"Good idea. Why didn't I think of that?" Beth paused and took a closer look at her. "Are you okay, Ruthie?"

"Yeah, just tired. I didn't sleep very well last night."

"What's going on with you and your cowboy? Everything okay?"

"Yeah, he's amazing."

"He is something. Don't tell Lang, but I've always thought Harley was the handsomest man in Saguaro."

Ruthie smiled. "Have a great Mommy-daughter lunch."

***

She was just drifting off to sleep when he stepped onto the porch. His footsteps startled her and she opened her eyes. "Harley?"

He gazed down at her, eyes soft and loving. "Hey, babe."

"What are you doin' here? It's the middle of the day."

"How are you feeling?"

"Fine. Stupid, but fine."

"I have a very important question to ask you."

She sat up, rubbing her eyes. "What is it?"

In answer, he knelt and reached into his pocket. "Ruthie Morgan, I love you. I may be a fucked-up mess, but I know one thing for sure. I cannot live another day of my life without you, in my home, in my bed, and all the rest of it. You mean everything in the world to me. Will you marry me?"

Tears streamed down her face.

"Hey, baby, I'm not that bad, am I?"

"No, you're the most wonderful man in the world and I love you so much."

"Is that a yes?"

She nodded as he reached up and wiped her tears away.

"Well, then, I want to give you this," he said, opening a small blue velvet box. "It reminded me of you, but if you don't like it, we'll exchange it for exactly what you want."

She stared wide-eyed at the lovely ring, a light blue sapphire surrounded by tiny diamonds in an antique setting. "Like it? I love it and I love you!" She threw her arms around him.

"And there's more," he said after a long, lingering kiss. "I don't want to wait and get married in three, four, or six months. It's not the pregnancy and you showing. I just don't want to spend another night without you as my wife."

"What are you saying?"

"We can have a party if you want it, whenever you want, but I want to get married today, just you and me. I've got a justice of the peace booked for five and dinner reservations at the Red Mesa. If you don't want to tell anyone yet, I'll bring you home after dinner and we'll have the honeymoon when you're ready. Anytime, anyplace. What do you say, babe?"

"Well, yes, of course, I'll marry you today," she said, kissing his cheeks, neck, and lips. "We'll have a beautiful dinner and lots of kisses and then spend tomorrow night together planning our honeymoon. Oh, Harley, I can't wait!"

She beamed her beautiful smile, and he drew her close. "Okay, babe. Can you be ready by four thirty?"

"With bells on. I love you, fiancé."

"I love you, too, baby."

CHAPTER 57

"So our head wrangler is finally taking you on a proper date?" Leonora said as Ruthie stepped onto the terrace.

"Ha, ha."

"Pretty dress, darlin'," her father said, smiling up at her. *She's happy,* he thought. *Happier than I've seen her in a long time.*

"I would have preferred a more modest look for a first date," her mother said, eyeing her. In truth, she looked glorious. The summer dress in a swirling blue pattern matched her eyes, the skirt flouncy, bodice snug, revealing just a little cleavage. The strappy white sandals showed off her pretty legs and as she twirled. *Finally, our baby looks happy. I wonder what's going on?* Leonora thought.

"That's my cue," Ruthie said. "Have a wonderful evening."

"You too, dear," Helen said. "You certainly look lovely."

"Yes, you do," baby," Leonora said. "And don't be too late. Remember we've got your father's big secret doo tomorrow."

Behind her mother's back, Ruthie caught his eye and winked. "Don't worry. Some of us have to work before the big doo."

Harley whistled as she strolled toward the car, her skirt swishing in the breeze that came through the Valley in the late afternoons. "You look beyond amazing, babe."

"You, too, fiancé," she said. And he did, in an olive-green summer suit, beige shirt, and colorful tie.

They said their vows in Justice of the Peace Abe Parson's front parlor, his son and wife as witnesses. When Abe pronounced them man and wife, he drew her close and they kissed long and deep. Finally, Abe chuckled. "Hey, folks, looks like you're ready to start the honeymoon!"

His wife offered them cookies, but they thanked her and walked out into the sunlight arm in arm. "Hello, Mrs. Langdon," he said, turning to kiss her lightly.

"Hello, husband," she said, kissing him back. "Harley?"

"Yeah, babe?"

"I'd like to keep my own name. Will that bother you? I mean, in private you can call me Ms. Langdon or anything you want, but—"

He kissed her forehead. "It's fine, Ms. Morgan."

"Are you sure?"

"Absolutely. You hungry?"

"For you."

He smiled, the soft smile that was hers alone. "Later, babe."

***

He had reserved the terrace at the Red Mesa, a private enclosed space ringed with flowers and trees, with a single table set for two. When they were ushered in, she stood looking around, eyes wide with amazement. "You know, I've lived here my entire life and never been in here."

"Me, neither," he said, smiling. "So we're discovering it together."

After Josh, their waiter, brought drinks, seltzer for her and a beer for Harley, he took their order and disappeared. As the door closed behind him, they were enveloped in the quiet beauty of the secret garden.

"Happy?" he asked.

"Deliriously. I don't suppose we can lock that door?"

"Patience, my bride."

"I'm sorry we can't share a bottle of champagne," she said, clinking her glass with his.

"After the baby's born we'll come back and share the most expensive bottle they have."

"Be careful, cowboy. They have a pretty pricey wine list."

"Anything for you, babe."

"Thank you, my love, but I'm putting a hundred-dollar cap on it."

"Done," he said, clinking her glass. "You feeling okay?"

"Pretty good. These crackers are helping."

"Have I told you how much I love you?"

"Yes, but tell me again."

They spent the dinner talking about the farm and what her father had shared about his and Spark's plans. As they shared a creamy caramel flan ringed with berries from Ruthie's Morgan's Run gardens, he said, "We agreed to wait on a lot of it until they broke the news, but it's a pretty big operation. Because of their wish for secrecy, they had Spark's architect from Portland draw up initial site plans, but I know he wants to involve your brother, Sam, in the actual building plans. Aside from the barns and stalls, there are to be a number of cabins. They've got Spark"s contractor, Kevin Larrabee on board."

"He told me about Kevin. So here goes another Morgan-slash-Foster extravaganza. Those two like everything big, and Dad likes to keep the people he cares about close by and employed."

She put her spoon down and reached across the table, taking his hand. "Harley, I know Dad and Spark want to build you a house, or build a general manager's house."

"Yeah, but I've given it a lot of thought, babe. If it's all the same to you, I'd rather plan and build our own house. If your dad won't sell us land, we can start looking around."

She smiled. "You read my mind. That's exactly what I was going to say. And I'm pretty certain Dad'll find some parcel he's willing to part with."

A little while later, Josh slipped in and returned the check, wishing them a good night.

Ruthie sighed. "I don't want this evening to end."

Harley stood and reached out his hand. "You've read *my* mind, babe. Come with me, my beautiful wife."

"Did you tip Josh to lock the door behind him?"

"Better than that." He led her to the opposite side of the garden and threw back French doors that opened into a lovely room lit by candles on every surface, the floor and white coverlet of the four-poster bed strewn with pink rose petals.

She gazed around, eyes wide with amazement. "You are a man of many surprises, dear husband of mine."

"Damn straight. Now, pretty as you look in that dress, babe, let's get you out of it. I want to make love to my wife." He closed and latched the French doors, slipped off her dress, and led her to the bed, laying her down softly. "What's your pleasure, Mrs. Langdon?"

In white lacy bra and panties, she lay gazing up at him. "Much as I love it all, can we get close, really close, right now?"

"Your wish is my command," he said, undressing, then gently slipping off her remaining garments.

As he entered her, Ruthie cried out, arching up to meet him. She ran her hands up and down his strong, hard chest. "I love you, I love you, I love you," she said, giving herself to him fully and completely as they took each other to the moon and back.

The second time was long and languid as they nestled side by side, eyes locked throughout simultaneous, tumultuous orgasms that left them peaceful and warm. When they finally dressed to go, it was close to midnight. As he opened the doors, she held him back. "Kiss me one more time so I know it's real."

"Oh, babe, this is real, alright. Realer than anything else I've ever done in my life."

CHAPTER 58

True to his word, Spark's limousine buses arrived to pick up picnic goers midmorning at the Lodge and winery. They'd also added a few extra stops along the way. Since camp was in full swing, those personnel with the exception of Amy, Maggie, and Ben all stayed on the job. The farm workers drew straws and all but a couple came. The winery closed for several hours. Jaybo Dillon was not feeling well enough to attend, but Martha, Neecy, and her husband, Manny, all came along.

Some attendees drove their own vehicles in order to return as soon as possible. These included Harley, Nick Parker, Maggie, and the winery manager. Aria Fiorelli and her Portland catering crew, flown in for the event, went separately in three smaller vans. The catering team had been on site working since dawn. Kevin Larrabee, the general contractor, and the workers Spark had brought from Portland were also coming.

Leonora had insisted that the entire Morgan family, and Maggie's dad, Ned Williams, ride in one of the buses with car seats installed for the kids and baby Lily. She now presided over her brood as they made the thirty-minute drive. "This had better be good, Ben Morgan. Don't make me regret marrying you all those years ago."

"Don't worry, darlin'," he said, putting his arm around her shoulders. "Even if you're not thrilled, we'll have a nice family drive and a picnic."

"Pish tush. We could do that and stay home."

"What, and ride around the ranch ten times in our fancy limo buses?" Kyle said, elbowing Ruthie, who rolled her eyes.

Always prone to carsickness, Ruthie did not enjoy riding in the back of the limo. *Do not let me throw up! What a way to feel for our big announcement!*

Kyle leaned forward, tickling baby Ben. "Hey, anyone got some Dramamine? Shortcake back here looks carsick. Some things never change."

Her father looked back. "You want to switch places with your brother?" he asked, referring to Ben, who was in front seat beside the driver.

"Thanks, Dad. I'll be fine. We're nearly there, right?"

"'Bout ten more minutes."

"I'll make it, I'm sure."

Soon they turned down the dirt road, heading west. In the last week, the road had been graded and smoothed, and crushed stone laid. After a mile, they took the side road that led into the huge stretch of green that seemed to go on for miles. The graders had almost completed work on the first track oval, but the only structure on the property was a huge white tent erected for the picnic. Spark's other buses had arrived and Aria and her crew had laid tables with sandwiches, salads, appetizers and desserts. Bars were set up on either side, and a small stage had been erected in the middle of the tent. At the center of the stage, a large object stood covered with a drape.

Leonora stared, mouth agape. "Oh, my Lord, Ben! What have you done?"

"Wow, Dad," Robbie said, "Lemme guess. Golf course?"

"I'm guessing the Morgan-Foster Amusement Park," Kyle said.

"I can't believe it, Dad!" Beth said.

Ben laughed. "For two old geezers, you and Spark have some wild hobbies!"

Leonora swatted his shoulder. "Don't call your father an old geezer."

"Seriously, Dad, this is amazing," Sam said, "golf course, park, or whatever."

Lang and Rose nodded their heads.

"Oh, I wish Jaybo had come," Martha Dillon said. "It's so beautiful and you know how he loves wide-open spaces. I can't believe you got grass like this to grow even here in the Valley. We are still in the Valley, right?"

Ned Williams, who sat between his daughter and Emma, whistled, pretty certain of what he was seeing in front of them.

"Ned? You know something! What do you think this is?" Leonora said, frowning as she gazed over at him.

The handsome wrangler raised his hands, but said nothing.

Ben Senior smiled, listening to the chatter. "Okay, everybody out! We're the last bus so all will be revealed shortly. Everybody head to the tent and Spark and I will make our announcement so we can eat, drink, and be merry."

As they made their way under the tent, Ruthie caught sight of Harley standing with Jeb, Amy, and Toby. He turned and they locked eyes. The intimate moment was interrupted as her mother caught up with her.

Leonora grabbed her arm. "Ruthie Ann, you were the only one of your brothers and sister who didn't seem surprised back there."

Oh, boy, here we go. "Mama, I was carsick, if you recall."

"Well, did you know?"

"Of course not," she lied, breathing in the cool, fresh air and beginning to feel a little better. *If she ever finds out, there'll be hell to pay.*

"Humph," her mother said. "You got home awfully late last night and we didn't see you at breakfast. How was your evening?"

"Fine, nice. Oh, look, Mama, Dad and Spark are already on stage!"

As her mother went scurrying off to catch up to Helen and Martha, Ruthie found Harley. He, Jeb, and Amy had been joined by Ben, Maggie, and their children. The rest of her siblings, including Hope Seymour, Robbie's fiancé, stood nearby.

Harley touched her hand and she laced her fingers in his, smiling up at him. She glanced over in time to see her brother Ben nudge Maggie. *Of course Nosy Parker noticed. I have no secrets, no privacy in this family! Well, I don't care. Before we leave here, they'll hear a secret they haven't managed to ferret out unless Abe Parsons and his family ignored our pleas and got on the Valley hotline.*

CHAPTER 59

Dapper in summer-red chinos and an open collared blue dress shirt, Spark cleared his throat. "Welcome, everyone."

"Those are two silver foxes, aren't they?" Kyle said.

"And don't they know it?" Ben said, receiving an elbow from Maggie. She frowned at him, then turned her attention back to the stage as Spark put his arm around her father-in-law's shoulders.

"I'm so proud to be standin' here with my college buddy, the two of us provin' that you're never too old to begin somethin' new. You're now lookin' at the start of a dream we've had since our Stanford days."

"Oh, my goodness, Ben, you haven't!" Leonora cried, the truth dawning.

Her husband raised his hand. "Hold off a sec, darlin'."

Spark grinned at her. "Leave it to Nora to remember those nights of drunken talk and grandiose plans. Truth is, we've both done pretty well for ourselves. Now we have the means and motivation to bring our dream to life. Ben, if you'll do the honors?"

His friend pulled off the drape with a flourish to reveal two large easels, one holding a sign and the other a large board with the Portland architect's initial site plans. "Welcome to Saguaro Valley Stables! Sign won't go up on the road for many months 'cause we're keeping this quiet till we get further along. Breeding and training thoroughbred race horses is a very competitive business. Buddy, you want to take it from here?"

"We're hoping to be up and running a year from now. We'd be happy to answer a few questions, but this is a party, so we old windbags don't want to wait much longer to enjoy the incredible spread Aria and her team have prepared for us. Come check out the site plan, which is only tentative, because we're hoping our resident architect will take it from here and design the buildings and final layout. Does anyone have a burning question before we eat, drink, and celebrate?"

Leonora stepped forward, hands on hips. "Well, I certainly hope that you two old fools are not planning to run this?"

Her husband laughed. "We didn't get to where we are by bein' that stupid."

Spark grinned, nodding his head. "Rest easy, honey. We're the capital guys and, as you know, we've got plenty of it."

"Then who?" she asked.

Realization suddenly dawned on her oldest son's face and Ben looked over at his best friend, who looked as if he'd rather be in Timbuktu.

"We've tapped homegrown expertise to be our general manager," Spark said, "and I'm happy to report that my buddy here used his extraordinary powers of persuasion to convince a certain wrangler to stay in the valley instead of hightailin' it to Napa."

As all eyes turned to Harley, Ben Senior said, "We are enormously grateful to Harley Langdon for negotiating his way out of his contract with Hayworth Ranch and to agreeing to take this on. We can't think of a better person for the job. He's also been a true gentleman in honoring two old men's wishes and keeping our secret until today. It was an unfair request, but he accepted it with grace and good humor. We welcome any and all expertise, advice, and opinions, and we'll need you all, but it will be our general manager working with the contractors, architects, and workers who will build Saguaro Valley Stables. Spark and I have feelers out for the horses. Just this week, we closed the deal on several fine animals, and we're pretty excited about that. As we keep building, we're gonna need a lot of expertise there."

Spark stepped forward. "Harley, would you like to say a few words?"

Harley blushed scarlet and raised his hands. "I'm great—this is your show, guys, I will just say that the men standing up there have given me a tremendous opportunity for which I am humbled and grateful. I will try my darndest to live up to their expectations."

Ruthie watched him, so proud of her husband. She wanted so badly to throw her arms around him. As Ben Senior raised his hands and said, "Okay, everybody, let's eat, drink, and be merry" she did just that. They were soon surrounded by people congratulating him, shaking his hand and patting him on the back.

As the crowd dispersed to get food and drink, Kyle Morgan approached him. "Are you guys planning to have a resident vet?"

"Absolutely," he replied. "And you know the job's yours if you want it."

Maggie came round to hug him, smiling, her eyes bright. "Oh, Harley, I'm so pleased for you and so glad you'll be staying in the Valley."

"I'm gonna need you, partner. With the horses and all. Parker and Jeb, too. Not that I'd poach anyone, or be allowed to poach anyone, from the ranch."

"You've got us," she said.

"Sure have," Jeb said, shaking his hand.

His best friend waited until the crowd died down and his baby sister was distracted with the kids before approaching him. "Hey, buddy, great news." He grabbed him in a bear hug.

"Thanks. I hated not telling you, man."

"Hey, the geezers drive a hard bargain. That's why they're where they are today. Let's eat!"

As the group moved toward the buffet tables, Ruthie came to his side, whispering, "I'm so proud of you, husband of mine."

"Thanks, babe." He took her hand, eyes soft as he gazed down at her. "I'm the luckiest man in the world."

"Me, too. I mean, woman, of course. I've been thinking, my love. If it's okay with you, I'd like to keep the baby a secret for a little while. Would you be disappointed?"

"Course not," he said, squeezing her hand. "You know I want to shout it from the rooftops, but we can wait as long as you want."

"Good. Now can we get some of that West Coast food? I'm starving."

CHAPTER 60

As desserts and coffee were passed, he leaned over to her, whispering, "Hey, babe, I think it's now or never. Spark and your dad are making noises about winding down, and I've gotta get back soon if you want to go away tonight."

"Okay. You want to tell it or shall I?"

"It's your family, babe. Besides, I think I've reached my quota of public speaking today, don't you?"

"Okay then, let's do it!" With that, Ruthie popped up and grabbed a spoon and glass, clinking them together. Harley rose to stand at her side.

"Attention, everyone! Before people leave, we have an announcement."

"Yes!" her oldest brother said, slapping the table.

As Maggie shushed him, Ruthie continued. "As I was saying, we don't want to steal Dad and Spark's thunder, but Harley and I," she said, taking his hand and gazing up at him with love so plain that everyone could see.

"We were married yesterday," he said.

"I can't believe it!" Leonora cried.

Her husband grinned from ear to ear. *Hallelujah, our baby is finally happy!*

"Abe Parsons married us," Ruthie said. "We love you all very much, but it was something we wanted to do privately. We hope we can have a party to celebrate someday, but we didn't want to wait." She reached up and put her arms round his neck. As he bent to kiss her, the crowd cheered and clapped.

Immediately, they were swamped by congratulations and hugs and kisses.

"You're a sly old fox," Ben Morgan said, hugging his friend. "Have you got any more surprises?"

"Oh, you guys," Maggie said, embracing them as her children hugged their ankles. "I am so, so happy for you!"

"Yay for Auntie!" Emma cried as her brother jumped up and down.

After the commotion died down, Harley found Ruthie. "Hey, babe, I gotta move. We still on for tonight?"

She leaned against him. "What do you think? I only wish I could come with you now."

"Pick you up at five?"

"Perfect."

He kissed her, then turned to go. "I love you, babe."

"Me, too," she said, waving.

As everyone moved toward the bus, Beth grabbed her. "You're pregnant, aren't you?"

"How did you?"

"Maggie and I guessed. Oh, Ruthie, I couldn't be happier for you both!"

Ruthie hugged her. "So much for keeping that quiet. There's no privacy in the Morgan world. It's actually a miracle that Dad and Spark kept their secret so long."

"Don't worry, sis. Our lips are sealed until you want to tell people. And by the way, you better never let Mom know that you knew about the thoroughbreds. She'll kill you and Dad."

CHAPTER 61

He knocked on the Big House door at five and Leonora answered, giving him a hug. "Congratulations, son! I couldn't find you before, but I'm so happy for you both."

He smiled down at her. "Thanks, Leonora."

"It was a shock, but now I'm used to it. Besides, Ruthie's dad and I have always said there'd be no one else for her but you."

"That's for sure," Ben Senior said, hugging him. "Come in, sit down. Got time for a drink?"

"No, sorry, Dad," Ruthie said, catching them in the hall. "We'd love to, but we have dinner reservations. This is our honeymoon, after all."

"I suspect this is night two of the honeymoon," her mother said, "but go on, scoot! Helen's leaving in the morning, so say your goodbyes now."

Her cousin rose from her chair in the living room and came to give them each a hug. "Congratulations again, you two! I hope to see you soon."

"Count on it," he said.

Ruthie nodded. "One of our longer honeymoon ideas is a trip to Martha's Vineyard. That's near you, right?"

"Not too far. Let's just say I'm on the way. I have a lovely guest room if you'd like to visit."

"Scoot now, you two," Leonora said. "We love you!"

***

"You gonna tell me where we're going now?" she asked as they headed through town.

He turned to her, a big smile on his face. "Well, we had such a great time last night, I asked Josh to book us for tonight. We get the terrace and the room and they'll serve us anywhere, any time."

She scooted over beside him, grateful for the truck's front seat as she kissed his neck and stroked his penis now straining the fabric of his new jeans. "Well, husband of mine, pretty as the terrace is, if it's all the same to you and Josh, I vote for the room. They can bring the food and close the door, and it will be just us all night."

"Sounds good to me, Ms. Langdon," he said, "but if you don't watch those hands and lips, we may never get there."

Huskily she whispered, "Is that a dare, cowboy? 'Cause as you know, I'll take you anywhere and everywhere."

"Sounds good to me," he said, pulling off into a wooded area, partially hidden from the road. "Scoot over, babe," he said. "And if you're wearing panties under that 'fuck me' skirt, you'd better hand 'em over."

Immediately, she sat up, straddling him, guiding him between her legs, slick, wet, and warm as she welcomed him. "You know me better than that. I ditched them back in town while you were pumping gas."

Hands cradling her soft, gorgeous ass, he pulled her closer as she rode him hard and deep. "I love you, Ruthie Morgan. If you don't kill me with this, I promise to love you more and more every day."

"I love you so, so much. Love me, Harley, love me, love me, love me! Oh, oh, oh! Never, ever stop!"

He smiled, watching her body suffused with the warmth of their lovemaking. "I'm with you, babe. Every step of the way, I'm with you!"

Please read on for chapters from ***Widow's Island!***

WIDOW'S ISLAND

Biologist Ned Fielding leaves the tattered remains of his marriage behind to spend six months on Winward Island, a property shared by SENCA, his land conservation group, and the reclusive Widow Barlow. Dispatched to the island to study a rare species of carrion beetle, Ned finds himself much more interested in studying the island's only other human, the beautiful Addie Barlow, whose screams of terror awaken him in the dead of night.

A hurricane and near drowning throw the island's two inhabitants together, and they begin a smoldering love affair. The locals call the Widow Barlow a witch and enchantress. They claim she murdered her much older husband, the philanthropist King Barlow, but Ned cannot quite believe the wild tales about the gentle woman he adores. Enchantress, maybe—with her closest companions an osprey, a dolphin, and a coyote—but murderess? Will Ned's quest for the truth destroy their love and break Addie's heart?

CHAPTER 1

"You can't send that nitwit Peterson to do the job. Jesus, Marty! The last census we sent him out on was so fucked up it had to be completely redone."

"Then who do you suggest, Phil? Margot's on Block Island till August and Ray's wife'd never cut him loose for that long. Six months is a long time to be away from the family. That's why Andy'd be so perfect. No wife, no kids, practically no friends, and—"

"Forget it. I'll call Ned. He's the best person for the job, anyway."

"Fielding? You gotta be kidding! Penny'd never let him out of his cage for six months!"

"Penny's got nothin' to do with it. They're separated."

"Too bad. I didn't know. Not that it's a surprise; mismatched couple of the century, if you ask me. Mrs. Society and Mr. Limpet. Geez, how'd they ever hook up in the first place?"

"Married when they were kids; baby already on the way. Some people grow up together in those kinda marriages. Some don't. Anyway, Ned'd be glad of the chance to get away, I'll bet. It's been pretty nasty on the home front, from what he tells me."

"Still under the same roof?"

"He's lookin', but they're still sharing the house. She's away right now with orders for him to be gone before she gets back. His family's house, too. 'Bout the only thing he brought to the marriage and Penny wants it. Sickening when you think of all the Pardington millions she has to throw around."

"Good old Ned. Penny's always been a bitch."

"Marty, I haven't got time for this right now," the older man interrupted, feeling like a traitor for gossiping about his friend's marriage. "I'll call Ned and if he can't go, better start packing. Someone's gotta be on the Winward Island by the middle of the month. *Nicrophorus americanus*, if they're there, will be emerging by then, and we want a complete study covering the whole six months till dormancy."

"I'll be in Portsmouth if you need me. Later, Phil."

Phil couldn't remember Ned Fielding's phone number and didn't keep a Rolodex or an address book. His blotter, where the number was jotted down, was buried under a mountain of papers. Shifting the pile back and forth several times, he peeked cautiously underneath each corner. As he moved toward the middle of the blotter, he started a landslide of bills, flyers, and grant proposals. The pile picked up steam, scooping up an overburdened vertical file in a downward rush. "Shit!" he muttered, watching the last of the papers cascade over the floor, some coming to rest under the water cooler, others floating into an open aquarium. "Sorry, Boris," he said, lunging to remove a stack of Chace Point Bird Sanctuary brochures from the back of a baby snapping turtle, too startled by the sudden onslaught to snap at him.

Turning back to the desk, he spied Fielding's number scribbled on the now-emptied blotter. He dialed. Busy. Leaning back, he closed his eyes for several minutes. It had been a hard year for SENCA, the Southeastern Natural Conservation Agency, of which he was president. The whole region was in a recession, and state and federal funding had been slashed. The first thing to go had been Phil's secretary, Edna, who had been with him since the beginning—almost twenty years. They'd been good years, he reflected. He missed Edna. Actually, she'd been ready to retire. He could easily hire part-time help, but he figured he'd save money, and besides, he hated to break in a new person and have her poking around in his and Edna's stuff.

SENCA was in better shape than most. They had a generous endowment. Lots of folks remembered them in their wills and the money had been invested prudently. King Barlow's gift alone would keep them in operation for twenty or thirty years. And in addition to the money, he had bequeathed Winward Island—half of it, anyway—to the agency in his will. The island had been the one holding they had neglected, until now.

On an unauthorized day trip, a couple of college kids, SENCA volunteers, had discovered what they believed to be Giant Carrion beetles, *Nicrophorus americanus*, on the island. A rare species of burying beetles, *Nicrophorus americanus* had been thought to be extinct until their discovery in recent years on Block Island. Now they might also be present on Winward. The importance of this study dictated that he must send a decent researcher. Ned Fielding was overqualified for this type of field study, but the only man within the agency whom Phil trusted to do the job right.

They hadn't sent anyone to the island since its acquisition twelve years earlier. It was time to conduct a complete census of the plant and animal life, time to map it out and give the island the attention it deserved. Its location along the Atlantic Flyway alone made it an important, extremely valuable acquisition.

He tried Fielding again. This time the phone rang four times before Ned picked it up.

"Ned, hey, it's Phil."

"Hi, Phil!"

"How are things going?"

"'Bout the same. You know about Penny and me. There's not much more to say."

"It's been great having your help at Chace Point this spring. Wish we could pay you more, but…"

"Hey, I've enjoyed myself. Ray and I just got the nest platform up on the spit—East Marsh—and we're lookin' for a new project."

"That's the reason I'm calling. You got a place to live yet, buddy?"

"I think I've got a place out near Watuppa Pond—friend of a friend. Gonna rent for a while till I get things straightened out. Why?"

"Well, if you're free to get away for a while, I have a job for you. Winward Island. Ever heard of it?"

"Yeah, off the coast near Derryville. Barrier island. We own it, don't we?"

"Yup. One of our few undiscovered frontiers. We need a complete census, soil samples, beach study, and surveying. Giant carrion beetles have been found out there, you know."

"No, I didn't. Wow, after Block Island, that should be…"

"Let me qualify my statement. Grad students *may* have found the beetles last summer. They took some pretty amazing photos. No samples, though. Just pictures. Only there a few hours. Typical. But listen, buddy, if the beetles are there, we could work with the Block Island people on a recovery plan to bring them back. We need you for that, Ned. What do you say—you game?"

"Sounds good. How much time you talking about?"

"At least six months, maybe more."

"Phil, I'd love to, but…with the divorce and all, I'm not sure I could get away for that long. Can I get back to you later?"

"Sure. I can give you a couple of days, but don't wait too long, buddy. Someone's gotta be out there by the middle of the month, and I'll have to get Peterson or Ray if you can't."

"I'll let you know tomorrow. Thanks, Phil."

Chapter 2

Ned debated an hour or two before calling Penny at the beach house to which she had retreated—until he "vacated her home." They had been living apart emotionally for so many years, a few extra months wouldn't hurt before their ties were legally severed. He just didn't care anymore. Didn't care if she took the house, the antiques, the dog. Although he would miss Haggardy. Penny didn't even like Haggardy. She was keeping him for spite.

"I can't believe how selfish you are, Ned. But then you've always put yourself first, before me, before the kids, before your social obligations, before everything. For God's sakes, couldn't you think of me just this once? How am I going to get on with my life if you leave me dangling here for six months while you're off counting bugs?"

"Do you want to get remarried right away, Penny?"

"Are you kidding? After what you put me through, I'll never marry again!"

"Then what does it matter, really? Six months isn't long after all the years we've—"

"Don't even say it, Ned! I will not have our estrangement become public knowledge. In fact, I'm having Martin draw up gag orders to that effect. I will not have my reputation ruined by gossip, and I'll thank you to speak to no one about our affairs, past or present, until the papers are drawn up."

"Penny, relax. Everyone knows. It's not exactly a surprise. Can we just let it go for now? I'm going to Winward and I'll be back the end of October, beginning of November. We can sign papers then, or if you can't wait, I can come back for a day to take care of things whenever you and Martin have documents ready."

"What about the settlement? What about all the details, the division of property?"

"You handle it, Pen. Whatever you think is fair. Have it all if you want."

"Isn't that typical! Once again, I have to do it all. Isn't there anything you want?"

"My clothes, tools, and—"

"Here it comes. I knew it."

"Well, if you'd like, I could take Haggardy. He's a—"

"Forget it! Just forget it, Ned! I wouldn't dream of sending Haggardy to some godforsaken island, probably loaded with deer ticks and fleas! Besides, he belongs to me."

"Fine, Pen. Listen—I gotta go. I'll send you an address where I can be reached and I'll call the kids, too. Not sure about email and phone access on the island, but I'll let you know."

"That's the other thing, the children. Are they supposed to wait six months, too, to have this settled?"

"I'll call them, Penny. If they have strong objections, I won't go, okay? Now, I've really got to go."

"Fine, I'm late for an appointment! You'll be hearing from Martin soon. Goodbye."

She clicked the phone down before he could say goodbye. Anything to get the last word.

He put off calling the kids until the evening, but he called Phil and accepted the job. He knew neither Ned Jr. nor Sydney, his daughter, would care, but he'd check with them anyway.

CHAPTER 3

Icy pearls of sunlit water fell noiselessly from the paddles as the kayak glided through the channel rounding the east end of Winward Island. With spring, Addie spent her mornings, just after sunrise, paddling in the marshes. A net and several empty burlap bags lay ready, stuffed in the prow beside her feet, should they be needed. But pleasure, not work, drove her to the sea in the early morning hours.

The day was clear and crisp. The April morning air embraced her with cloying chilliness. The marsh beckoned, reaching out to envelop her in its magical green depths, however thoughts intruded, distracting her from the rustling beauty. Usually she paddled hard for a time, then lifted the oars and drifted, listening to the sea birds screeching and calling, the fish jumping, and the swishing sounds of spartina, soft and soothing. Today she paddled ferociously as if driven by unseen demons, faster and faster until beads of sweat dotted her brow and her arms burned with the strain of exertion.

Her home was about to be invaded and there was absolutely nothing she could do about it. For twelve years, she had lived alone on the island. Now her sanctuary, her peaceful world was to be taken over, perhaps forever. Who would they send? Would there be more than one? Would they disregard the boundaries and trespass onto her side of the island?

The trustees of her husband's estate had assured her the conservation agency that shared the island with her would respect her privacy. They owned thirty acres, she twenty. The island was to be kept as a wildlife sanctuary. No building, no camping, no human habitation was planned for Winward Island, the name they had given it upon taking possession. Now they were sending someone to live for six months on her island. Six months!

She knew she was lucky to have the land at all. So many times over those last months, King had threatened to take it away, threatened to will the entire island to SENCA and let them have her cottage, her gardens, everything. He'd laughed and taunted her continuously, knowing that Winward was her only refuge, her only love. She didn't love him, had never loved him. But King Barlow had died suddenly, before he could change his will, and his widow had inherited the cottage and its surrounding acreage, the fields, ponds, gardens, and thicket. She also owned the cove with its many caves hidden beneath the cliffs, where she loved to explore.

The dock was in the cove, the only easy access to the island, hence the reason SENCA had contacted her in the first place, to request permission to use her dock. Recognizing the futility of refusing, she had written back giving her consent and requested that they use the west footpath to reach their property, rather than the more direct route running north to south, which traversed her fields. The reply assured her that the agency would respect her privacy, keeping to the western footpath when venturing forth from the dock. "Rest easy, Mrs. Barlow," the letter had ended. "Our people will try not to pester you in the slightest way. We are as eager as you are to ensure that Winward remains undisturbed and peaceful. Please contact me personally if there is any problem whatsoever. Phillip K. Bodington, Director, SENCA."

The letter from Mr. Bodington had not reassured her, especially the part about "our people." Was there to be a whole bevy of scientists crawling over the island for six months? Would there also be a steady stream of visitors taking part in the study? Visions of boatloads of college students descending upon Winward made her shudder, and the paddle jabbed unevenly beneath the glassy surface of the water, the handle nearly jerking free of her grasp.

Glimpsing a crab, its broad swimming legs catching the sunlight as he paddled sideways through the eel grass, she swung the net, a flawless extension of her right arm, and scooped him up, wetting the burlap bag with her left hand as she tossed him in. The action appeared to be almost reflexive, after which she continued paddling, worries consuming her still.

After an hour's time, she headed back, a bag full of crabs, heart and mind no lighter, but resigned. Dropping the crabs in one of the pots near shore, she paddled in and pulled the kayak up onto the beach. She kept her fishing scow tied to the dock, but she preferred to drag the lighter craft up onto the beach. That way it could be more easily carried to higher ground if a storm threatened, or she could drag it over the ridge for use in the pond near the cottage. She scanned the surface of the water closely for some minutes before turning to head up the path lined with rose hips and honeysuckle.

As she entered the thicket, she heard a familiar screech. She turned in time to spy a huge bird dropping from the vast blue above her, its talons outstretched as it fell. Pulling a leather glove from her pocket, she slipped it onto her right hand, stretching her arm out straight to her side. Sharp talons dug into the leather as the osprey came to rest, grasping her gloved hand. "Gwydyon, son of Don." She smiled, stroking his feathers. "How goes it with you this fine day?"

The fish hawk bowed his head, enjoying the attention, alternately gazing from his mistress to the sea. "I have nothing for you this morning. Maybe later." As she talked, she walked slowly along the path through the thicket. When it became clear that no meal was forthcoming, Gwydyon became restless. "Just a minute, my friend," she cooed, quickening her pace.

He was vulnerable to attack in the thicket, so she hated to release him lest his flight be checked by an unforeseen enemy. Without food, he was probably safe, but there were several golden eagles and great horned owls that frequented the island. While they rarely challenged Gwydyon on the open water, they might hazard a skirmish in the brush, where his sharp, lashing talons were less effective.

Finally, she reached the open fields. From there, the path ran straight through the meadows to the shingled cottage just visible in the distance. The bird arched his wings, rearing back, and Addie released him with an upward thrust as his powerful wings carried him aloft. As soon as he reached a safe height, he circled once, screeching farewell, and disappeared over the treetops toward the open sea.

Walking on, she stared ahead at the whitewashed cottage, her home for the past twelve years. Built seventeen years earlier, at the time of her marriage, the cottage had been winterized when Addie had settled permanently on the island. It had two stories, with a wide porch wrapped around its front and sides. The faded, white-shingled walls were alive with climbing greenery. English ivy crept high under the second-story windows and intertwined with clematis vines, the blue and white flowers not yet in bloom. The vegetation at first gave the impression of wild abandon, belying the hours of cultivation and care that made their existence possible.

A two-story barn with a lean-to shed and greenhouse attached stood behind the house to the south. The land gently sloped from the back of the cottage so that the taller, more imposing barn faded gracefully into the receding landscape rather than overwhelming the much smaller house. Its brown, weathered sides blended comfortably with the woods to the east, at harmony with its surroundings.

As she approached the cottage, a yelp of greeting hailed her as a tawny beast bounded up, flinging her front paws around her mistress. Laughing, Addie knelt beside her pet, ruffling the soft fur on the animal's back. "Aran! So you finally decided to wake up! No swim for you this morning?"

Woman and beast went together into the cottage, where she fed her pet, fixing tea for herself. Sipping it slowly, she sat at the worn table fashioned with her own hands from wood carted back from the mainland by boat. There was a salvage yard in Derryville she visited when she needed materials for the house, and she kept an old pickup truck on the mainland to use for these infrequent sojourns and for her deliveries of produce and fish. She hated driving, but as her client list had grown, the truck had become indispensable. The drop-off spots along the river reached roughly half of her customers; the rest had to be delivered by truck.

During the spring, her days were freer; the garden was not yet in full flower and the fishing still sparse. The Massachusetts climate demanded caution in planting fragile, warm-weather crops, but her tomatoes, peppers, eggplants, and flowers were flourishing in the warm moisture of the greenhouse. She tended to them first, passing among the rows to give water and pinch back unwanted growth. The greenhouse, too, had been built entirely from salvage materials. Unlike the cottage and barn that her former husband had had built as a wedding gifts to her, the greenhouse and shed had been constructed later on, after she had come to live on the island.

The first years she had survived on the small inheritance King had left her, tending a tiny garden for her own needs. When she began fishing, clamming, and lobstering to earn money, she expanded the garden, too. Once she began marketing her produce, she needed a hothouse. Rather than hiring someone to build it, she had undertaken the project herself. It had saved money, but more importantly, it had given her confidence and a feeling of self-sufficiency. Previously she had called upon plumbers, carpenters, electricians, and mechanics when things broke and needed repair, but since the completion of the shed and greenhouse ten years earlier, not another soul had set foot on the island. Whatever expertise she required came from books, the Internet, and her own experimentation.

Midday found her weeding and picking early spinach. She had already harvested parsnips and winter carrots, and her broccoli, cauliflower, and lettuces were well underway. She protected the lettuces at night and when the days were particularly cold, but the thick layer of mulch and the protected enclosure of the garden kept the plants relatively safe from a killing frost.

Until June she sold little of her produce, as most of her clients were seasonal residents who came to spend the summer at the beach. She had a few year-round customers who paid to have anything from her garden yield, as well as a share of her catch. What little money she made before June, however, came from the fish she sold to wholesalers. From June to October she sold only to her regular customers, unless there was a surplus. When summer cottages on the mainland coast were boarded up, she slowed down and moved into her winter schedule.

As the years went by, her customer list grew until she finally had to turn people away. She kept a waiting list of would-be customers only too eager to receive her weekly bounty, some offering double or triple the usual charge to be put "on the route." Addie refused to grow bigger, however, since the thought of having to hire help was abhorrent to her.

Each customer received three deliveries a week of fish, vegetables, herbs, flowers, and fruit. They paid a flat weekly fee, the same no matter what they received. When a new customer was taken on, they filled out a form with likes and dislikes. At that time, they selected which plan they desired: only fruit and vegetables; all five items—fish, vegetables, fruit, herbs and flowers; or just fish and flowers. While she attempted to cater to individual tastes, Addie brought a variety of offerings depending on what was ripe or what she'd managed to catch or dig or net on any given day. No one had ever complained, and the woven baskets brimming with fresh food were always a delightful surprise.

When the Widow's baskets arrived, dinner was planned around the bounty within them, whether it was steamers and corn; wild raspberries, apples, and blue crabs; or lobsters, arugula, and fresh scallions. Always there were flowers from early spring on—first tulips and daffodils, then iris, lupine, and wild sweet peas, then the zinnias, asters, cosmos, marigolds, coreopsis, snapdragons, dahlias, cornflowers, and all manner of wild flowers that grew in riotous profusion in Winward's meadows.

This morning would be spent repairing her lobster traps in preparation for the following week, when they would be baited and set out for the first time. She also needed to make several new baskets as she had reluctantly agreed to take on four new clients this year. Some of the old baskets were worn and split, in need of repair. Fashioned from rushes, dried in the sunroom over the winter, the baskets were strong and water-resistant, their large willow handles smooth and comfortable to hold, even when they were heavily laden with produce. Along with the baskets, she sometimes used burlap sacks for her deliveries if she was bringing large quantities of shellfish.

Each customer was allotted two baskets and several bags per season, the empty ones to be returned with the following delivery. If a basket was lost or misplaced, she had begun charging for new ones. Some people feigned loss in order to have one of the simple but beautiful baskets to take home at the end of the season, so she was careful to set aside enough of the cattails and rushes for drying in order to replace worn or "misplaced" baskets. Several times customers had suggested that she might like to sell some baskets to the local gift shops or stores in the city, where, they assured her, she would make a handsome profit. Addie always declined.

As she went about her afternoon chores, she began to relax. They would stay on their side and she would stay far away. She knew every inch of the island and every hiding place. *Six months and they will be gone.*

About the Author

M. Lee Prescott is the author of dozens of works of fiction for adults, young adults, and children, among them **Prepped to Kill, Gadfly, Lost in Spindle City (Ricky Steele Mysteries), A Friend of Silence, In the Name of Silence and The Silence of Memory (Roger and Bess Mysteries), Jigsaw,** and **Song of the Spirit,** and her newest contemporary romance series, **Morgan's Run,** of which **Ruthie's Love** is the sixth! Three of her nonfiction titles have been published by Heinemann, and she has published numerous articles in the field of literacy education. Lee is a professor of education at a small New England liberal arts college, where she teaches reading and writing pedagogy. Her current research focuses on mindfulness and connections to reading and writing. She regularly teaches abroad, most recently in Singapore.

Lee has lived in southern California (loved those Laguna nights!), Chapel Hill, North Carolina, and various spots in Massachusetts and Rhode Island. Currently she resides in Massachusetts on a beautiful river, where she canoes, swims, and watches an incredible variety of wildlife pass by. She is the mother of two grown sons and spends lots of time with them, their beautiful wives, and her amazing grandchildren. When not teaching or writing, Lee's passions revolve around family, yoga (Kripalu is a second home), swimming, sharing mindfulness with children and adults, and walking.

Lee loves to hear from readers. Email her at mleeprescott@gmail.com, and visit her website to hear the latest and sign up for her newsletters!

http://www.mleeprescott.com/

Follow me on BookBub at https://www.bookbub.com/authors/m-lee-prescott

A Note from the Author

I am thrilled to bring you Ruthie and Harley's sizzling love story! This marks the sixth of the **Morgan's Run** books, with more coming soon. Thank you so much for reading it. These beloved characters will be around as the series continues to grow. The Morgan's Run books are set in the gorgeous American Southwest, an area of the country that is dear to my heart because it is home to my youngest son and family, but also because its beauty is so extraordinary and so startlingly different from that of my New England home. What a backdrop for romance and adventure!

If you like **Ruthie's Love** and would be willing to write an Amazon review, I would be very grateful. If you would like to sign up for future book releases and occasional notices about my books, please visit my Author Website and sign up for my newsletter. I promise I will not share your address, nor will I flood you with emails. Do visit my site to read more about my books and hear what's next.

Finally, this book has been revised, proofed, and edited many, many times, but my intrepid assistants and I are human, so if you spot a typo, please email me at mleeprescott@gmail.com and I will fix it. If you'd like to know more about my other books, please scroll ahead to the next section, which is followed by sample chapters of **Widow's Island**, a sexy, stand-alone romance in my **Well-Loved** series.

Warm wishes,

M. Lee

OTHER BOOKS BY M. LEE PRESCOTT

Contemporary romances and mysteries by M. Lee Prescott include:

The Ricky Steele Mysteries

Book 1: Prepped to Kill

Book 2: Gadfly

Book 3: Lost in Spindle City

Book 4: Poof!

Also featuring Ricky Steele:

Jigsaw

Roger and Bess Mysteries

Book 1: A Friend of Silence

Book 2: In the Name of Silence

Book 3: The Silence of Memory

Contemporary Romances

Well-Loved Romances

Widow's Island

Hestor's Way

Morgan's Run Romances

Book 1: Emma's Dream

Book 2: Lang's Return

Book 3: Jeb's Promise

Book 4: Rose's Choice

Book 5: Hope's Wonder

Book 6: Ruthie's Love

Young Adult Historical Romance

Song of the Spirit